SILENT SHADOWS

Jennifer J. Morgan

Books by Jennifer J. Morgan

2022 Finalist - American Fiction Awards
Mystery/Suspense and Cozy Mystery (*Shadows in the Forest*)

2024 Winner - International Impact Awards
Best Fiction- Cozy Mystery (*Shadows in Alaska*)

* * *

Libby Madsen Cozy Mysteries

Shadows in the Forest
Spa Shadows
Shadowed Treasures
Shadow Retreats
Spooky Shadows
Shadow's Christmas Wish
Festive Shadows
Shadows in Alaska
Shadows Over Thanksgiving
Ghostly Amethyst Shadows
Silent Shadows
The Christmas Fairy - a holiday novella

SILENT SHADOWS

Libby Madsen Cozy Mysteries, Book 11

Jennifer J. Morgan

Secret Staircase Books

Silent Shadows
Published by Secret Staircase Books, an imprint of
Columbine Publishing Group, LLC
PO Box 416, Angel Fire, NM 87710

Book layout and design by Secret Staircase Books
First trade paperback edition: December, 2025
First e-book edition: December, 2025

Publisher's Cataloging-in-Publication Data

Morgan, Jennifer J.
Silent Shadows / by Jennifer J. Morgan.
p. cm.
ISBN 978-1649142320 (paperback)
ISBN 978-1649142337 (e-book)

1. Libby Madsen (Fictitious character). 2. Romantic suspense—Fiction. 3. Arizona—Fiction. 4. Amateur sleuths—Fiction. 5. Women sleuths—Fiction. I. Title

Libby Madsen Cozy Mystery Series : Book 11.
Morgan, Jennifer J., Libby Madsen cozy mysteries.

BISAC : FICTION / Mystery & Detective.
813/.54

To *my mother*—
Thank *you for all the guidance and support you've always given
me. I'm a better human, mother, wife, and friend today for it. I'm so
proud to be following in your footsteps.*
I *love you endlessly.*

PROLOGUE

(Fall 2008)

Pine trees blurred past as their Jeep jostled down the winding dirt road, leaving a thick brown cloud in its wake. Anyone following would be blinded by the dust.

The drive stretched on forever, especially after staying up all night celebrating. Their elopement had been perfect—only the two of them, no family drama. They'd agreed on that much; this fresh start deserved clean air, untainted by the complications of the past.

Soon, they'd be starting over.

A small town.

She gazed at him, her new husband, as he drove.

His head swiveled. "What?" he grumped.

"Nothin'." Her southern drawl lingered. "Just lookin' at you is all." The wedding band felt strange on her finger.

Two months from first date to marriage—like something from a fairy tale.

"Almost there," he said.

"Remind me how you found this place?"

"Friend told me about it."

The Jeep decelerated as he eased off the gas. She scanned the dense pines on both sides, searching for a turnoff among the endless trees.

"Jesus!" Her right hand shot up to grab the safety handle above. "You call this a road?"

"This is it." His knuckles bone-white against the steering wheel as his eyes fixed on something only he could see through the trees.

The vehicle crawled forward, jolting over roots and rocks.

She gripped the handle, not daring to let go. Her smile froze in place even as something cold slithered through the recesses of her mind—wasn't this what she wanted? Freedom at last—no more family drama, his or hers. They'd fantasized about escaping since their first night together. Now here they were.

"Are we close?" she asked, fidgeting.

His face darkened. "What difference does it make? We've left the entire world behind. I'm doing this for you!"

Her bladder ached as she glanced at her watch. After an hour of rough terrain, relief came when his left blinker clicked on. He veered directly toward a gate.

The sign mounted there—TURN BACK NOW— should have told her everything.

CHAPTER ONE

(Summer 2023)

I notice, scanning my computer, the schedule is completely full at Dharma Inspired Day Spa for the upcoming week. Normally, that would thrill me; however, it doesn't seem likely I'll convince my business partner, Lexi, that I could be away for the summer. It's a huge ask, and we need to have the conversation soon.

I sigh, close the lid on my laptop, and gaze over at Shadow resting peacefully on her bed in the office's corner. Despite wanting to curl up next to her for a rest myself, I stand and quietly exit the room, ready for my next client.

Knocking on the therapy room door, I ask, "Ready?"

Hearing the affirmative through the door, I slowly open and enter the room.

"Hey Libby!" Sage's muffled voice sounds perky this morning.

"Sage, it's been a while. Did you have an amazing time with your artist friends in Europe?"

A cute giggle escapes. "So much fun … it was beyond amazing."

"We've sure missed you here. Can't wait to hear all about it."

Sage has been a client of mine since massage school. Ever since, she's been my most devoted client, but more importantly, she is also one of my closest friends. My family even considers her one of their own.

Sage fills me in on her trip abroad—Italy, France, and Greece. She paints the picture so well—traveling with several artists, beginning in Italy, and taking a course from a renowned artist they all admire. I'd never heard of the man, but that's no surprise to anyone. My area of expertise is in the health-related field—I never studied art, nor do I have a single creative cell in my body. Sage has pestered me for years to join her beginner's courses she teaches. Although I know she'd be the best person to learn from, I've never taken her up on the offer. Maybe someday.

"I tell you, Libby, you have to come with me sometime," she said with a yawn, and then grimaced as I found the sore spot near her left shoulder blade.

"I wish! I've always wanted to travel overseas."

"Then do it."

"Yeah, mainly I've got to find the time and the money." I lower myself onto the tall stool nearest her head. Spreading oil across her shoulder blades, I lean back against the wall for leverage and use both of my heels interchangeably to slowly knead the tense muscles around her shoulders. "Feels to me like that long plane ride didn't do your body any favors?"

She agrees. "So, work has been busy then?"

"Very busy. It's surprising how many new clients we've added since that festival last year."

"That's great!" she manages between a couple more yawns.

"Absolutely. The only problem is that Greg has been called back to Heber for work this summer."

"Forestry work?"

"Yes."

"Oh, no. I thought he got permanently transferred here in the Phoenix area?"

"Yeah, he did. But the forest service is continually short-handed—so, that means he goes wherever he's called."

"At least it's not that far away. What is that—two hours or so?"

I nod, even though she can't see me with her face in the cradle. "Give or take. Yes, I'll get to see him on my days off. I'd love to spend the summer up there, though."

Drowsily, she mumbles, "Who wouldn't? With our temperatures here, I hear everyone heads up north for the summer to escape."

I shift my position and reach up for the bars, standing on either side of her torso, and using my left heel to work on her upper back. Hearing a gigantic sigh as she releases a deep breath, I get lost in my own thoughts.

Cool mountain air. The sound of the breeze through the pines. Enjoying the summer with my fiancé at his mountain home. I smile—the word fiancé is still foreign to me. We've been engaged for several months now, and I still haven't gotten used to my new moniker. I couldn't imagine what *wife* was going to feel like.

Sage's breathing slowed. Jet lag and the soft spa music had dropped her into a calm slumber. I gently continue the bodywork, wondering how I should approach Lexi on the subject of joining Greg in Heber this summer. Wondering *if* I should even consider it.

Over the past year, we've hired several new therapists because of the ramp-up in business. We have even talked about opening a new location. Both of us have been too busy to put much more thought into it, but that sparks another idea for me as I cover Sage's left leg and uncover her right one. As I methodically work the hamstrings, calves, and glutes, I consider possibilities for a pop-up location up in Heber. Shoot, maybe I can even do that from Greg's house? That would lower the overhead.

Soon, I finish with my friend's backside and need her to roll over. I hate to wake a peacefully sleeping client, but as I hop down from the table, she feels the movement and slowly lifts her head.

"Hey sleepy!" I whisper.

"Did I really fall asleep?"

"You sure did. Now, I need you to turn over. But don't worry, I'll cover your eyes with a soothing warm lavender towel, if you'd like."

"Mmmm, hmmm…" was the only sound she made.

At the end of the two-hour session, I delicately wake Sage, help her into the oversized fluffy robe, and guide her out to the Serenity Room, where she indulges in hot herbal tea and a warm flax muffin. She looks content sitting and listening to the gentle flow of the nearby fountain.

Before I get ready for my next client, I remind her, "Don't forget, we're all getting together this weekend before Greg heads off to the mountains. Hope to see you then."

"Definitely." She smiles and blows me a kiss.

Several hours later, Shadow and I make it home, finding Greg in the kitchen. The aromatic smell of garlic greets us as Greg pulls me in close.

"Lasagna for my fiancée?" he whispers in my ear.

Again, a faint tickle runs up my spine when I hear the word. "Absolutely! You made it?"

He blushes. "Well, no. I picked it up at our favorite Italian place in Apache Junction on my way home. It's reheating right now. Also, I'm toasting some garlic bread, and I put together a simple salad with what we had in the fridge."

My heart swells, and I plant a kiss on his lips. It's not long before Shadow worms her way between our legs, trying to separate us.

Giggling, I tear myself away from my delicious forest ranger and give Shadow a pat on the head.

"Jealous much?" he asks Shadow before turning back to the oven and peeking inside. "Almost done."

"Okay, I'd like to clean up. Do I have five minutes?"

He leans in closer to my lips and whispers, "However long you'd like, Ms. Madsen." After reluctantly pulling away from his lingering kiss, I manage my way back to the bedroom where I change into comfortable shorts and a t-shirt.

The table is set when I return, complete with lit, tall tapered candles and a bottle of Chianti.

"Wow, you've thought of everything. What's the occasion?" I reach out for my wineglass.

"Does there have to be one?" He grins, picking up his own.

I lift the glass and simply add, "To us."

"To us."

Savoring the delicious lasagna, I glance up and see a look cross his face. "What? Something wrong?"

He shifts in his seat, setting down his fork. I do the same when he reaches for my hand. "I really don't want to leave. It reminds me of early in our relationship, when we traveled back and forth so much to see each other. I guess I thought those days were behind us."

"Aww, it'll be okay. You won't be gone long, right? We'll figure it out."

"Well, that's just it. I spoke to Al today…"

"He's going too?"

Greg nods his head. "They informed him it's a summer-long job, possibly longer."

"And they didn't tell you that?"

"Not exactly."

I take another sip of my wine and start in on the salad while thinking about how to keep this positive. To date, we'd only been told *temporary* assignment. "I had an idea that came to me earlier at work…"

"Oh, yeah?"

"I'm not sure it's the best timing, or that Lexi will be in favor…"

"What is it?"

"Well, Sage had mentioned how many people from the valley travel to the high country during our long hot summers. What if I worked from up there—drumming up business for Dharma Inspired all summer?"

"Hmmm. That might fit right in with something I've been working on."

I set my salad fork down, raising my eyebrows in curiosity.

"You know how I have a couple of acres up there, right? I've been considering moving a modular home onto the property."

"Really? For what?"

"Well, initially, I was thinking of passive rental income while we're not using the place. I really don't want to rent out my home, but if I got the setup right, perhaps I could rent it to someone who could do some upkeep on the property."

I perk up. "Someone who could monitor the place when we're not using it … nice."

"I don't know. But one of my buddies is in the business—I've asked some preliminary questions, and I think it's doable. Depending on when we could get everything in place, maybe you could use it this summer for massage therapy. And, hey, when we have our wedding there in the fall, we'd have extra guest quarters for the family."

"Oooh, that's an idea."

"Let me make some more calls tomorrow. You talk to Lexi and let's see what works out. For tonight, let's enjoy our meal and then find a Netflix movie to watch."

"And that's why I love you—I love your ideas." A chuckle escapes at the same time I feel a warmth settle over my body. I'm so blessed.

CHAPTER TWO

By the time I finish my last session the following evening, I am utterly exhausted and still need to stop by my mom's house before I can rest at my own. I see Shadow across the room looking eager to get outside for a bathroom break and decide that definitely takes priority right now.

She's imploring me to hurry when I see the light on in Lexi's office.

"Oh, hey, I thought everyone had bailed on me," I tease, poking my head into her office.

My best friend and business partner glanced up, her eyes looking much more tired than normal. "Yeah. Just wrapping up—how about you? Almost ready?"

"Sure. Let me take Shadow out quickly and then I'll

grab my stuff."

The trip outside is very short as Shadow knows the routine and immediately runs to the end of the building to the dirt lot next door. As I reach the end of the sidewalk, she's already running back to me.

"What a good girl," I coo, reaching down and scratching behind her ears. "Come on, let's go see Grandma next."

I gather my laptop bag, some of Shadow's toys, and stuff them into my large tote bag, and shut off the lights. We step into Lexi's office.

"Did you have a full schedule today also, Lex?"

"Oh man, it's been a little crazy, hasn't it?"

"It's been great. Remember several years back during the pandemic, how scared we were we'd never keep the doors open?"

She nods as she reaches into her desk drawer, pulls out her purse, and then locks it up and stashes the key in its hiding spot. "I never want to be back in that situation. We're much better off overly busy, I'd say."

"Exactly. And I'd like to get back to the conversation we had about expanding—maybe adding a new location. Maybe tomorrow we can carve out some time to discuss?"

Distractedly, Lexi nods, ushers me out of the office and through the building to the front lobby. "We'll see. I really need to get home and get my guys fed before I have a mutiny on my hands."

Chuckling, I picture her husband and six-year-old son waiting for her with pitchforks as she pulls up into the driveway. Nothing could be further from the truth. I am sure my dutiful detective friend, JJ, has most likely fed Joshua already and has a plate still warmed for his lovely, hard-working wife. They were the epitome of a modern dual-income family who doted on their only child.

"Speaking of mutiny, my mom is probably holding dinner for me. Greg is already there, along with Jordan and her kids. I had best get moving along. We'll catch up tomorrow." I grab Shadow's leash as Lexi opens the front door and we hurry out to the car, leaving her behind to set the alarm and lock up.

I hear the squeals before I see the children. Shadow barrels through the front door the second I open it, and the kids go nuts. It's always good to catch up with my nieces and nephews—they have so many activities going on lately that it's getting harder to coordinate visits.

Jordan's oldest, Apple and Annie, now in their early teens, are constantly on the go with their friends, and each involved in their separate interests. I think I am busy, but I am truly mind-boggled with how my sister keeps up with her family. If it were only the teens, that'd be bad enough. But she also has two younger ones, Chase and Ryan. Chase is six and fully immersed in sports. Ryan turns three this summer—not fully potty trained, and also not showing any signs of leaving the terrible twos behind any time soon.

"Libby! It's about time. We were just getting ready to call you." My mother, Julia Madsen, crosses the room and sweeps me up into a giant hug. When she pulls back and holds me out at arm's length, she simply states, "You look exhausted."

"Good to see you, Mom. Sorry, I'm late. Such a busy day."

Greg comes over and gives me a peck on the cheek, whispering, "The oven timer barely sounded just before you pulled in. Don't stress." I squeeze his hand as my sister lobs a ton of questions at me.

"Your little spa doing well? Are all the people you've

hired staying busy? Are you profitable yet?"

"Whoa, Jordan!" I give her a hug, too. "Let me settle in first."

Mom rescues me with the call for all the kids to clean up and get to the dining room table.

I give Jordan a shrug. "Sounds like dinner is ready." She rounds up her children, corralling them into the hallway bathroom to wash hands. I linger, watching the scene: the teenage girls racing to be first, Chase slowly relenting but really wanting to play with Shadow, and then Ryan going into a full meltdown in the middle of the hallway.

Greg and I exchange glances. "Sure this is what you want?" I asked.

"Uh…" his eyes widen. "Maybe not four?"

I laugh, turning toward the kitchen. "Mom, what can I help with?"

She hands me the water pitcher. "Fill the glasses. Except for Ryan's sippy cup—he gets milk."

"Got it."

Updates about the kids' summer activities dominate the dinnertime conversation. When it comes around to us, Greg explains the forestry work he'll be doing on the Mogollon Rim for the summer, and I relate how much my thriving business keeps me busy these days. Mom catches all our attention by announcing she and Margie had a 'mystery trip' planned through their church.

"You don't know where you're going?" I ask, inquiring what a mystery trip is.

"Nope. They tell us generically what type of clothing will be required to pack—for warm weather or cooler temperatures. And soon we'll learn whether we're traveling by plane, bus, or train. But the destination is a mystery until the day we meet for the departure."

Jordan's expression sours. Her face squinches up as if she'd sucked on a lemon before she blurts, "*Why?*"

"Oh, c'mon, because it's *fun* … adventurous." Mom looks at me for backup.

Pointing my index finger at myself, I question Mom. "Me? What?"

"Well, I just thought you might support me on this. I mean, you two are adventurous. Doesn't it sound fun?"

"Oh. Yeah! Of course. I'd be game."

Greg eagerly agrees as well.

Jordan gives us both dirty looks, shaking her head. "I'd *have* to know exactly what the itinerary was before I paid any money for the trip. What if you hate it?"

Mom wipes her mouth with her napkin. "Well, I know several church members who have attended many of these trips, Jordan. They rave about them. I actually find it more exciting that we know nothing about the destination. Therefore, I have no preconceived ideas of how it'll go— sounds like so much fun."

"When are you going? How long?"

"Two weeks in July…"

My sister's voice takes a whiny turn. "But what about the kids? Remember, you usually take them."

"Honey, you and Pat are going to have to figure it out for the two weeks I'm gone. Margie and I are doing this trip."

Jordan's eyes cast down awkwardly. I realize then what her negative reaction to Mom's trip is all about. She enjoys working part time again for the first time in years, and the struggle of finding summer daycare for four children was real.

She quietly mumbles something about asking her ex-husband to take them for those two weeks. Ryan breaks the uncomfortable silence by tossing a piece of chicken onto the floor and then screaming when Shadow eats it.

"Maybe I could help?" I state.

Everyone, including the children, goes silent, staring at me.

"With what?" Jordan asks.

"Watching the kids." My mouth goes dry, and I rub my sweaty palms along my pant legs underneath the table.

"You?"

"Yes, me. Maybe I could fill in a little bit—take them to Heber when I go? Fresh mountain air would do them good."

All at once, the kid chatter begins again.

Chase shakes his head vehemently. "No! I hate fresh air!"

Ryan's sippy cup teeters on the edge of his high chair, and my mom quickly snatches it up. This causes him to screech, "MINE!" in the highest pitch I've ever heard.

Apple and Annie both talk excitedly at once, in unison.

"We'd *love* to spend time with you, Aunt Libby!"

"Can we bake? I'll bake for you all summer long!" Apple asks.

My mom was the first adult to call for order in her dining room. "Hey, family! One at a time, please…"

I hold my hands up in surrender. "Sorry, I didn't realize that it'd cause this much of a commotion. Really."

Jordan's eyes meet mine. "You'd be willing to do that? I never thought…"

"Yes, Jordan. I'm willing to help where I can. But we're going to have to work out the logistics. For one, I don't know exactly what my work schedule will be. So, work with Pat—figure out your kid's summer schedule the best you can first. Let me know specific dates and I'll see what I can do. Oh, and probably we need to juggle one or two kids at a time. I can't take all four."

"Sure, sure. Okay. Thank you, Libby. I—"

I clear my throat. "Never thought I liked kids? Well, you're wrong. I love my nieces and nephews and would be happy to pitch in and spend more time with them." As the words cross my lips, I seriously wonder what I'm getting myself into. Even Greg looks a little puzzled if I'm being honest with myself.

The rest of the evening goes smoothly enough. Although I eat way too much and call it an early night.

CHAPTER THREE

The benefit of being longtime friends, totally in sync with each other, is how you can practically read each other's thoughts. Or at least that's what I used to tell myself anyway. This morning, I swear Lexi is about to drop a bomb as she sits me down to talk. How did she phrase it? *We seriously need to talk.* It's not the words themselves, but the *way* she articulates them.

Alexis Johnson, the kindest human soul I know, normally embodies an unwavering, ethereal spirituality about her. Of course, she's a meditation instructor and full-on yogi, so I'm just saying that my decades-long friend doesn't rattle easily. In the only way *she* can, Lexi holds a steady stronghold over her own household, but in such a loving manner I never quite understand *how*. But that's

Lexi—she always has the same pragmatic, unbothered spirit, approaches life with optimism, and makes people feel seen. This morning feels different.

She moves quickly, energy buzzing around the room in a way I feel and see. She spins around, closes the door, as her flowing chartreuse caftan swirls around her thin, lithe frame. Pulling out the closest chair, she lands in the seat without her usual grace.

"I've been thinking…" she starts breathlessly.

I hold up a hand. "Wait. Is everything okay, Lexi?"

She takes a deep breath. Slowly she exhales, and there comes the gorgeous smile with sparkling white teeth, which seem over-whitened against her smooth cocoa lips.

"Libby. I'm sorry—it's been a morning already. Joshua informed me about a costume he needs…." She stops and smiles again. "Never mind about that. I've been thinking …"

My eyebrows shoot up, imploring her to continue as she takes another long breath in.

"I've been thinking that we should expand."

"Yes, we started talking about…"

She stops me. "Hold on. Let me finish. I *want* to expand, but I was looking at the financials and we're still not there yet. It doesn't seem practical."

"I…"

She held a hand up. "But I heard you talking with Bella the other day about how Greg is going to be working on the Rim for the summer…"

My eyes lift again, intrigued.

"And we both know how many of the valley's residents head north for the summer to get out of the heat. Maybe there's a way we can capture that lost summer business by opening a location up in Heber? Or Show Low?"

My lips part into a wide smile. We *are* so in sync.

"That's funny. You know when I asked to talk to you today? That's precisely what I was going to ask you. It's like you are psychic or something."

Her smile fades. She reaches her hand across the desk and pats mine. "I still haven't figured out how to get around the high overhead costs, though. I stayed up late last night trying to make it work, but with the salaries we've already added, and then renting space, utilities, insurance…"

"I might have a solution."

She's ready to tick off another item on her mental list and then looks up at me.

"Greg might have actually figured this one out."

"I don't understand…"

I fill her in on the idea of his guest home addition, and we spend the next twenty minutes brainstorming ideas on how we could manage my existing Mesa client-base amongst the current staff. After trying several ways, I feel a bit defeated. I certainly don't want to lose clients, but want to find a workable solution. *Maybe all this is a pipedream?*

Lexi's eyes find mine again. "Hey, if it's meant to be, it'll be. Let's give it some more thought and see what works out. The great news is that we've built a substantial business here, and discussions of expansion or pop-up locations are really cool to be talking about. Maybe if your summer location works out, we can consider some other locations around the valley, too?"

As she stands, so do I, and before she gets to the door, I come around the desk and wrap my arms around my friend.

"Thank you! And you're right—we'll figure it out."

By that evening, dragging myself through the front door, I find Greg at the stove sautéing shrimp scampi, and my heart lifts. He pours me a glass of Sauvignon Blanc and sets it on the counter. I plop down on a bar stool.

"I've got good news!" he exclaims.

"So do I…"

"Oh? What's yours?"

"Lexi is fully on board with my spending the summer up north. In fact, it was her idea!"

"Oh, really? Was all that preparation to convince her unnecessary?"

"Nope. The only problem is that I've got to find a reasonably priced location—that's the hard part. And since we don't know when your modular building will be move-in ready, I may not be able to go until later in the summer. Kind of defeats the point of spending summer in the mountains."

"End of May," he blurts out.

"What?"

"It's being delivered and installed in two weeks. Move-in ready by end of May."

I jump down from the bar stool, run around the countertop, and leap into his arms. "Are you serious?"

"Yeah, my buddy Ted came through for me. I put a deposit down today, and it's ordered." He sets me back on the ground and turns to give the scampi a final stir. "Let's eat."

"Oh, my goodness!" I pour more wine and quickly set the table. "I've got to call Lexi."

"Let's enjoy our meal first—and talk about life in Heber. Are you sure you want to spend an entire summer living the small-town life?" His chuckle reminds me of the first time I met the handsome forest ranger—his soft demeanor and those brilliant blue eyes that sparkle when he laughs.

I nod firmly, and I take my first bite.

CHAPTER FOUR

The month speeds by as I transition my clients between the other therapists at the spa. Greg has already been gone for several weeks, starting his new assignment, and taking delivery of the cabin-style modular home. Before I even know it, I'm packing a bag and gathering my mobile massage table and supplies for the summer move.

Shadow knows something is up. Bags being packed always means a fun adventure, and since we take her traveling wherever we go, her excitement level now is off the charts. The second I load her belongings into my 4Runner, she jumps in and refuses to move.

"Sweetie, we're not quite ready to go, and it's too hot for you to sit in the car waiting." As soon as I mention the word 'cookie', she hops out and follows me back into the house. "Good girl." I hand her several bites of a broken-up dog treat. "Now, what are we forgetting?"

She follows me throughout the house as I check all the doors and windows, and look around for last-minute items. After filling my water bottle, we walk through the front door and I lock it. Shadow runs right for her seat in the back of the vehicle, and I clip her seatbelt attachment into place.

During the two-hour drive, my mind races wondering if I'm making the right decision. Suddenly, it all seems so impulsive. Leaving my clientele? What if they abandon me over the summer? What if I am stuck all summer in a small town with nothing to do while Greg works?

Shadow's bark pulls me from that train of thought. I glance around to see what she is barking at and see we'd just passed a car with a large dog hanging its head out the window.

I definitely need to find something else to do besides massage work. First off, I have the work of painting and decorating my new guest house/ work space. That will keep me busy for a week or two. I'm sure there are other projects around Greg's property that can occupy my time, too. Plus, I'll meet new friends—I'd already met a few of his forestry friends last winter. Maybe their partners will want to go hiking or kayaking on the lake? I settle down as I come up with more ideas.

Pulling into Heber-Overgaard, I glance around, remembering how small a community it is. My previous time here only amounted to a couple of days in the wintertime, and other than sledding and snow-shoeing, we spent little time in town. Back when I first met Greg a couple of years ago on a search and rescue operation, I remember visiting the gas station, the library, and the hardware store. These points of reference are familiar to me as I drive slowly, looking for where I'm supposed to turn.

I find the turnoff and slowly make my way along small community roads. Winding past small rustic cabins and then fancier estates, I recognize Greg's modest-sized log-styled cabin.

"Oooh, look, Shadow. Back there, past the tree line a bit—there it is! The new place where we'll work. It's cute."

She's not paying any attention to me. She stands up in the seat and barks straight ahead, piercing my eardrums, seeing Greg outside on the front patio waving as we drive up.

Shadow wriggles wildly, but thankfully is stuck in her seat until Greg opens the passenger rear door and unbuckles her. She leaps out of the vehicle, jumping up and down, reaching Greg's full six-foot height.

He says, "Whoa, little girl, you sure are wound up," and holds his arms up to stop her from bumping into him. She takes off running in circles—up onto the patio, back down, and around several trees, then right back over to Greg for some love.

I grab my purse from the front seat, turning just in time to see a flash of black fur speeding around the vehicle and then plopping down again at Greg's side. "I think she remembers the place."

He pats her head and then leads us up the porch stairs, holding open the front door. "Welcome home, you two!"

As soon as I cross the threshold, he scoops me up in his arms and plants a long kiss on my lips. "It's been too long…"

Feeling his warmth settles all my earlier nerves; I am exactly where I need to be. "I agree."

Shadow's sniffing sounds distract us; we both laugh. Her nose was in overdrive investigating her surroundings.

He pulls away, and I see she has her snout at the baseboards, moving methodically throughout the great room—the living area, dining room, and the kitchen. She lingers longest in the kitchen before quickly darting back into the living room.

"I suppose we should get the car unloaded—and then I can't wait to show you the new guest house."

Before we make it off the front porch again, a construction truck pulls in behind my 4Runner.

"Ah, Ted … forgot he was stopping by today," Greg mutters to me. "I'll introduce you."

Shadow bolts over to the man's truck.

A sizeable man slides out of the cab and greets us with a friendly smile, reaching down to greet the exuberant Labrador. Then he looks up at us, and his rosy cherub cheeks glow.

"Libby! Good to see you again." The amiable man reaches out and gives me a bear hug.

"That's right. You two met over Christmas," Greg quickly reminds me.

Ted sniggers. "Briefly—I wasn't much up for the sledding y'all were doing. But the hot chocolate and camaraderie were fun."

"Good to see you again, Ted. I understand you helped Greg get our new guest quarters in place. Thank you so much!"

"Yep. Yep. It was a good deal—someone backed out of their contract last minute, and we saved a lot of money not returning it to the manufacturer. Greg called at exactly the right time. Worked out for all of us."

"So, you are in sales *and* construction?" I point to his vehicle.

Ted removes his ball cap, running his large fingers through his thick brown curls. "Libby, I'm an all-around kinda guy, that's for sure. Over the years, I have done a bit of everything."

"Including forest service work, too?"

"No, no. The rest of our gang do that type of work. I met Greg and some of the others when they worked the Rodeo-Chediski fire back in 2002. Remember that, Greg?"

"Boy, do I … that was the first forestry incident I worked on."

"You fought the fire?" I asked.

He shook his head. "Well, I was brand new to the forest service and in my early twenties when I got stationed here. Mostly I helped with area closures—actually, whatever was necessary to assist the firefighters, honestly."

"Oh, don't let this man downplay his worth. I knew from the moment he showed up on our front doorstep and helped my family evacuate, he's the real deal. Greg saved our lives."

Chuckling uncomfortably, Greg stops Ted. "I'm not sure I'd go that far. At least your family listened to the authorities and evacuated when told to."

"But you made sure all the right people were in place to take in our livestock … you found space for all our pets, too. And not only for my parents and siblings, but for everyone in our neighborhood."

"Just doing my job…" Greg shuffles his feet awkwardly.

We walk around the side of the house toward the new cabin, following Ted. It was my first full view, and my excitement grew.

"This seems larger than what you described," I mutter to Greg. "You said something like adding a *tiny house*."

"Well, it's eight hundred square feet—give or take," Ted explains. "You'll see, it's a perfect guest house. Or, er … Greg mentioned something about your work."

"Yes, I'm a massage therapist."

"Ah! Right … that's what I'm here for today. I'm installing crossbars." He stops while Greg pulls out the keys and opens the front door.

I step inside and see a decent-sized space with a small kitchenette and living area. Farther down a small hallway, there's a full bathroom with a walk-in shower, and then two more doorways on either side of the hall. I peek inside the first one and see a small bedroom—it looks like a queen-size bed and small dresser would fit fine. Across the hallway, and next to the bathroom, I step into another room. This is my new workspace, but I can see where it could easily double as a second guest room as well.

"So, this is where you want it?" Ted's booming voice startles me.

I was still taking in the room, but nod my head when I see him pointing toward the ceiling.

"Greg gave me the specifications for the rod and crossbars, so I can get started. Can I ask, though … why do you need such a sturdy wooden beam for massage?"

Laughing, I pull out my phone and quickly bring up a TikTok video showing Ashiatsu massage. As he watches the therapist holding onto the rod above her head, and then using her bare feet to massage a client's upper back, he blushes.

"You do that?"

I nod. "Yes, I do … wanna give it a try?"

He gets flustered, backing out of the room.

Greg and I laugh teasingly. "Don't worry, Ted, we will not trap you into it."

"Right. Yeah … I better go get my tools," he says nervously, bolting from the small cabin for his truck.

"He's a funny guy."

Greg agrees. "No one better than Ted—good people for sure."

I walk around the room, sizing up where I'd like to set up the massage table.

Greg opens a door that I assumed to be a closet, but it went to the hallway bathroom. "I thought this would be handy since you have to wash your feet before each session—all convenient for the client to use prior to the session, too."

"And accessible as a guest bath for either bedroom when used to host family. I can easily fold up my mobile table and store it in the closet when I'm not using it. Maybe we can get a Murphy bed installed here for guests."

"Oooh, I've always loved Murphy beds. Would you get one that has a sofa or maybe a desk and shelves? I think they come either way?"

Shaking my head slowly, I look from each wall and then back to Greg. "I'm not sure yet … I'll have to take a look. No idea what they cost, either."

"Of course. Well, you'll have fun getting it exactly how you want it. In the meantime, let's get you all unpacked and settled in. I've got to stop in at the office for a few hours, and then we'll meet the gang for dinner and drinks. Sound good?"

"Perfect." I stretch up on my tiptoes when he leans in for a kiss. "I'll try not to make Ted any more uncomfortable than I already have."

CHAPTER FIVE

Later that evening, we walk hand-in-hand into the local burger joint. Greg scans the crowd and finds his buddies sitting at a large table toward the back of the room. We wind our way through the tables.

"It's hopping in here for a Monday. Guess the summer crowd has already begun to fill the campgrounds and seasonal rentals."

In the corner, I see a burly man stand up and recognize Ted in his beige plaid long-sleeve button-down shirt and his jean overalls.

"Over here—we've got two seats along the wall here." His chubby cheeks flush as he guides me where we need to go. I scoot down the bench in the crowded corner booth. Greg shakes Ted's hand and goes around the table greeting the rest of his friends.

"Remember Libby?" he asks the two couples at the far end of the table from me and points in my direction. They nod and wave.

I wave back, smiling and saying hi as I recognize them from our short winter trip.

"And Libs, the gentleman on your left—that's the top dog, Mark Rogers, and his wife, Juanita. Across from them, of course, you know Al, but you haven't met Toni yet. We all call her Taz." The entire table chant in a deep tone, *Taz*. "And her partner, Beth."

"Wow, I hope there isn't a test later," I chuckle as laughter erupts. "Good to meet you all!"

The server approaches and takes all our drink orders. I notice Ted already has a beer in front of him as he orders another one. The rest of the table insist the margaritas are the best in town. With that recommendation, I go along with the crowd.

I lean forward to get Toni's attention.

"Seriously, Taz is what I go by…" she reiterates when I call her Toni.

"How did you get that nickname?"

Greg interrupts, "If you saw her on the job, you wouldn't have to ask that question."

She and Beth chortle.

Beth hollers over the ever-increasing volume of the voices in the room. "Trust me, it's killing her to have to sit still this long for dinner."

Al chimes in, "There is no slowing Taz down. From dawn to dusk, this woman is a machine out there."

Taz, with her short, slicked-back dark hair and piercings in eyebrows, nose, lips, and lining both ears, sits back, taking it all in. Clearly, she's used to the attention, and I sit enjoying the show. Taz wears a black tank top, her brown skin glowing beneath numerous colorful tattoos. Beth's arm is around her shoulders, pulling her girlfriend in closer, and then playfully taking her knuckles to Taz's head. They laugh at the guys telling their tales about her.

"We may not have the Tasmanian Devil in North America, but on the Mogollon Rim, we have our own sort of Taz!" The group hollers to that, lifting their drinks and cheering on their teammate. She gives it back to the guys as much as she takes it—all in good spirits.

Beth pushes aside her shoulder-length blonde hair and leans forward. "So, what do you do for a living, Libby?"

"I'm a massage therapist."

That gets the table's attention and simultaneous "oooohs."

I ask Beth the same question and learn that she's a woman of many talents. She volunteers, it seems, everywhere she can, including the local community center. But to earn a living, she also works as a customer service representative remotely from home. In addition, she's an artist—most of her work is in clay sculpting, but she dabbles in painting, arts and crafts projects, and has written several novels as well.

"Where do you find the time to do all that?"

Taz chimes in. "Maybe I'm not the only super energetic person in our household?"

We all chuckle, and I watch how lovingly they support each other. I notice the wide variety of interests they share as they open up and give me a glimpse into their lives.

Glancing down the long table, I see everyone talking in small groups. That's the trouble with large groups in crowded restaurants; it's difficult to engage with everyone. But as I sit back, taking it all in, and trying to stay engaged in what Taz and Beth have to say, I feel enormous gratitude. I sense new friendships blooming and look forward to my summer in the mountains.

I hear Beth ask, "Maybe you'd like to volunteer?"

I nod slowly. "Um, sure…"

"We do this firefighter charity fundraiser annually—it's so much fun. With a silent auction and everything! It's a really big deal around here."

I smile, trying to remember if I've ever participated in a silent auction before. "However I can help, I'd be happy to."

By the end of the evening, I had signed up through Beth to help the firefighters with their annual fundraising event. I also handed out business cards to everyone and had several in the group promising to book massage appointments soon. More importantly, all of them knew someone who was sure to schedule with me.

When we get in the truck to drive home, I have Greg remind me of who everyone was at the opposite end of the table.

"I wish I could have visited more with them. Maybe we can have them over for a barbeque or something?"

"For sure. Don't worry, you'll have all summer to get to know everyone."

We pull up in front of the house and my heart swells seeing the golden glow of light through the windows. I feel right at home already.

The next morning, Greg leaves before daylight. Shadow and I sleep in a little longer, but at first light, I lace up my trainers, grab a jacket, and put the dog's harness (we call it a bra) on. It takes nothing for me to convince Shadow to head out for a run.

The crisp mountain air invigorates all my senses. Back in the valley, the early mornings are already too hot for running. I savor the cool air on my face, even though my ears and nose become quite chilly. Shadow's nose is busily sniffing everything we pass, but I keep the leash taut, not allowing her to pull me aside. She's doing much better these days. Now that she's nearly three, and search and rescue trained, handling her on the leash goes so much more smoothly. I remember several times when she pulled me down, or I nearly tripped over her.

We stay on the dirt road until it comes to a fork. Not knowing the area too well yet, I am hesitant to take too many turns or get too far away from home. As I contemplate, I hear a vehicle approaching and pull Shadow off the road. Just in time, too. The black truck speeds by, kicking up dust and loose rock as I turn my head away.

Shadow barks, staring into the cloud of dust.

"Maybe we should just head back." I guide her to the other side of the road, and we start running again, heading back to the house.

I make a mental note of taking the 4Runner out later to familiarize myself better with the area. Not only that, but I'd love to find an area for trail running. Surely, Greg could point me in the right direction.

After a nice, long shower and a light breakfast, I'm ready to meet up with Beth and learn more about this charity event. I give Shadow a cookie for her kennel and feel horrible about leaving her. Looking into those big brown eyes—*how does she do that?* She is accustomed to coming to work with me every day; this is unfamiliar to her.

"I'll be right back. It won't be long. Then we'll get back to decorating our treatment area."

Whether or not she accepts that explanation, I sneak out while she crunches on her dog treat.

Pulling up at the community center ten minutes before our agreed meeting time, I find loads of people around, and I go looking for the blonde-haired, blue-eyed woman I met last night.

"Libby!" I hear from across a large room as I step inside. Beth uses both arms and waves them wildly while doing a little jump in the air. I wave back, picking up my pace. I see now what everyone mentioned last night about her energy level. And yes, it's probably similar to the one they call Taz—I'm guessing that's what makes them a perfect couple.

"Hey Beth … I feel like I'm late," I mention as I check my watch. "Everyone's already busy doing stuff."

"Yeah, I figured I'd get here and get everyone started first. That's why I had you come at ten. We started at eight."

"Oh. Well, I'd have been happy to …"

"No, no. This way, I have time now to show you around, make some introductions, and get you started on receiving silent auction items. I should have asked whether you have an SUV or a truck?"

"Yep, a 4Runner."

"Excellent. I'll be sending you to our storage facility later. Since there are other events here at the community before the firefighter's, we won't be able to store much onsite. Plus, you won't believe the number of donations we've received—they keep coming in."

"Cool ... let's get started."

Soon, I meet several community center leaders, the head of the firefighter's union, local chapter, and the mayor herself.

"Okay, over here in this room, I'm going to have you help Willow intake all the silent auction donations. You two will log, label, and transport everything to the storage unit." She barely catches her breath before we arrive squarely in front of a slight woman bent over a large wooden box. She stands abruptly, appearing disheveled.

I'd describe Willow as being in her late thirties, similar to me, fashioning athletic wear, cute pink and purple Brooks trainers, and her long brown hair pulled up into a messy bun. She looks up at me with a look of utter confusion.

"Libby, this is Willow. Willow, Libby is going to help you catalog the donations and get them transported."

Willow appears friendly as she reaches out with her thin hands to shake mine, her voice soft and firm. "Good to meet you, Libby. Always good to have help."

Beth hurriedly excuses herself and leaves me with Willow.

"Can I help with that?" I ask my new volunteer partner.

She struggles for a second and then looks up at me. "Yeah, I guess. If you could get on that side." She points, and I move around the sizeable crate. "Now, let's see if we can lift it."

I bend my knees, secure my hands beneath, and then on the count of three, we slowly raise the heavy object from the crate and onto a table.

"Wow! That's gorgeous." I walk around the table,

examining it from all sides. It's a sculpture made of varying materials. Metal—I'm guessing bronze was one, but there are wood components as well. Not having an ounce of knowledge about such things, my eyes take in the intricate design of a horse lying down on the ground, with its head raised and ears pointed high. An enormous wooden traveling trunk, with equally detailed features, rested right next to the bronzed horse. I lightly touch the trunk, finding it has a smooth texture. Between the solid piece of dense wood and the heavy metal, I see our struggle was real. Hefting it from its container was no easy feat.

"This is a real blessing," Willow states softly.

I lift my eyebrows in question.

"The great artist, Pat Schellinger, donated this to us."

"Oh! I'm not familiar with his work."

"Not him, *her…*"

I nodded slowly. "So, it's valuable then?"

Her eyes widened, and then, with a purposeful bob of her head, I have my answer. "This will bring us all the money we'll need for the fundraiser—just this one item." She looks on proudly, admiring the art piece.

"So, what do we do? Beth said something about logging…"

"Oh, right. Yes." She turns around and grabs a clipboard. "Here, you jot down what I tell you."

She rattles off some codes, and I fill them in on the form before she hands over a sheet of peel-and-stick labels. I notate the artist's name and today's date.

"Oh, and for the form, what's the minimum bid?" I inquire.

"Ten thousand."

"Whoa! Really?"

"Yep."

I complete the form and then double-check that the label is legible. "Where do we stick this?"

"On the bottom."

Both of us grimace, then go to the horse end of the piece, grunting as we tilt it. "You got it? I've got to release at least one hand," I ask.

"Yup, but hurry."

I quickly reach out with my right hand and peel the label from its sheet, sticking it on as quickly as I can. Gently, we set it back in place.

"Okay, now we're going to have to put it back in the crate."

I scan the room, looking for some hefty guys. "We should get more help, don't you think?"

"I suppose you're right. It's going to be more difficult to lower it in without damaging it."

"Maybe we finish up labeling the other donations first? Someone may show up who could help."

"Good idea."

She shows me the next box of items. We log and label gift baskets of goodies, handsewn and decorative items, books, local business gift cards, antiques, and the list goes on and on. Minimum bids ranged everywhere from one dollar to the whopping ten-thousand-dollar item. *Would anyone really bid that much? In this tiny town?*

By the time we wrap up our duties, it looks like I have made a new friend. Turns out, she appreciates me even more when I find help to complete our final task. A couple of volunteers, local high school football players, safely lower the art piece back into its crate and also help us load it into the back of my 4Runner. The best part is that they agree to tag along to help us unload everything at the storage facility.

When that's done, Willow slams the back end shut and wipes the dust from her hands right onto her jeans. "We made good time doing all that—how about lunch at the bakery?"

"Sure. I'm starving now."

She nods, and we load into our vehicles, and I follow her to get lunch.

CHAPTER SIX

Word of mouth helps bring in my first few customers to my Dharma-Inspired pop-up location. Of course, Willow, my first new mountain friend, is my very first client.

As I patiently wait in the living area of the cute new guest quarters, I admire the soft earth tones I've painted the walls. I kept it simple—a sofa and loveseat combination along with an area rug, some indoor plants, a ladder shelf in the corner and then a few wall hangings. Everything I found was from a thrift store, except the sofas we got at a neighbor's garage sale.

I glance at my tablet, reviewing the information Willow filled out ahead of time. No medical conditions I need to be aware of. I check the clock at the same time I hear her say she's ready.

Slowly, I open the door and find her in place on the massage table, with her face down in the cradle.

"Are you comfortable?"

"Oh yeah. This is really nice. But—it will not hurt, right? Walking on me and all…"

I can't help but chuckle as I walk around the table, adjusting the sheet and brushing oils on her. "First, I don't walk on you—so please don't worry." I take a moment to explain exactly how it works. "Speak up at any time if the pressure is too deep."

"Oh, I will!"

"Hey, I also noticed on your form—your last name. I hadn't known it until now. Springs—Willow Springs."

"I know, I know—the lake down the road from here. If I had a nickel for everyone who pointed that out."

"No connection or story there, then?"

"Nope. I was born and raised in Mississippi, and best I know, my parents had never been to Arizona. So, no, I don't believe there's any connection."

I hop up onto my stool at the head of the table. I place my heels on her shoulders and gently roll them across and down to the blades.

"Oh, wow. That is something."

"Too deep?"

"Oh, no … absolutely perfect."

I continue checking in with her as I listen more to her story of growing up in Mississippi. She has two siblings— her younger sister, Joanne, and an older brother, Mike— with whom she rarely connects anymore. He was seven years older and moved away while she was still quite young. He had a beef with their parents when he left and never engaged with the family at all. She says her dad told stories, ranging from Mike running off with some cult to being a drug addict. She also explains how she'd heard different versions from distant relatives—that their dad was particularly hard on him and had revised the history to suit his own needs. Willow explains she never could figure out exactly what those needs were, but she and Joanne certainly toed the line after what'd happened to Mike. At least until Joanne, who was a few years younger than herself, suddenly moved out at sixteen. Again, the stories abounded, but Willow also moved on with her own life. None of the siblings maintained much contact after that, until recently.

I find it common for clients to prattle on, telling their life stories on my table. Oh, the tales that have been told! Most of the time, I tune out a lot and add in a small 'mmm, hmm' here and there. In other circumstances, I've come to know my clients very well by the things they've divulged to me during these tabletop confessions (the term that Lexi and I came up with).

Today, I am interested in Willow Springs' history. Over the past week, we have worked closely on the charity work, gone to lunch several times, and she's come over to join us, along with a couple of Greg's friends, for dinner at our house. It feels like a developing friendship. After having said there was little contact with her family, she drops an interesting fact.

"Joanna will actually be here tomorrow. Had I mentioned that already?"

"No, I didn't know you two were in contact. I'd love to meet her."

"Oh yeah, you will. I'm looking forward to it—I haven't

seen her in years. She's going to help us with the fundraiser. Sheesh, we've put in all this work already, but there's more to be completely ready by this weekend. So much more to do!"

"Is there really? After all we've cataloged? How many items are in the silent auction?"

"Well, it's not *only* for the auction, you know—this event goes on for the full Fourth of July holiday weekend as well. Then afterwards there's the church back-to-school fundraisers that'll get into full swing."

"Oh. I wasn't aware of that."

"Yeah, at the community center, we do it all."

I remember Beth mentioning something about problems with retaining volunteers. *Was this why? Had they all become burned out with one event after another?*

After I finish Willow facedown, I hold up the privacy sheet and ask her to roll over onto her back. Adjusting the cover, I brush more oil on and secure the sheet, only exposing her legs before I stand back on the table and continue working my bare feet on her quadriceps.

"I've got to get Joanne in for one of these massages. What did you call this again?"

"Ashiatsu."

"Yeah. She'll love this. I've never had anything like it—you know, I'd never in a million years have known you were using your feet."

"I'm happy you're enjoying it."

Afterward, we cross through the overgrown grass to find Greg on a ladder. I hadn't heard him return, so it's a surprise when he shouts out, "Hey there, ladies. What are you up to today?"

Willow shouts, "Best massage I've ever had!"

"Oh good! All ready for the firefighter's ball?"

Willow smiles, craning her neck to look upward. "Well, I think we're ready for the fundraiser—though the ball at the end has never really been my sort of thing. You know, getting all dolled up and dancing. Eh."

This was the first I was hearing about a dance.

"You ladies heading over to the community center?"

I nod. "Yep, gotta grab my purse first. Should I leave Shadow here with you?"

"I'll be leaving here again shortly."

"Alright. I'm sure Beth won't mind. She enjoyed having her around there yesterday."

I leave Willow and Greg chatting while I run inside. Soon we're on our way, and I follow Willow into town. Shadow leaps out eager to greet Beth, who's standing at the back door with her clipboard, when we arrive.

"Ah, we have extra help again today!" she exclaims.

Taz appears from inside the building, immediately drawn to Shadow. Kneeling down, she showers my dog with attention. "I just love Labradors. How old is he?"

"*She's* turning three this year."

"Wow, very well behaved. They're usually more rambunctious, aren't they?"

I agree and tell her all about Shadow's search and rescue training. She's a great puppy, but since she's my first Labrador, I can't attest to 'normal' behavior.

"So, what's on the agenda today? Don't tell me there's more donation items to be logged in?"

Beth shakes her head. "No, no. I think we've got all the donations ready. In fact, so many that we can host several community fundraisers before we'll run out. Today, we'll be making all the final preparations for the big weekend."

Taz interjects. "First, we need a few things from the storage facility. Since you've got the keys, Libby, would you mind running over there?"

"Not a problem. Anything heavy? Do I need a partner to help me lift?"

Taz pulls a sheet of paper from the clipboard. "No, just these few items…" She instructs me on where I'll find them in the large storage unit, and Shadow and I load up into the 4Runner and take off.

I pull into the now-too-familiar U Box It Storage. The place is enormous—it has always surprised me how much stuff people store, and I wonder how often they actually *use* what they stash away.

I navigate the 4Runner around several turns before coming to Row C, which houses the double garage-sized units the community center rents. Pulling up slowly, I shift into park and tell Shadow to stay while I go inside. She doesn't appear happy with that instruction.

Rifling through my purse for the keys, I can't find them. I check the console—nothing. Again, I search through my bag. Finally, I discover they'd slipped into an inner pocket. Pulling out the familiar metal keyring, with the community center's logo emblazoned on it, I toss my purse back onto the passenger seat and shut the door. Shadow shifts in her seat, hoping I'd changed my mind. Her whine sounds like, "Why?"

On the keyring are several keys. I walk up to the padlock and, of course, the first key I try doesn't fit. Patiently inserting each key, I strike out with every one of them.

"Oh, c'mon…" I hiss, losing patience.

Again, I try each key—none of them work. Finally, I call Beth but she doesn't answer. Willow answers her phone, and I ask if she can hunt Beth down and get me a set of keys; I must have the wrong ones. Then, I sit inside the cab with Shadow until I see my friend's truck. She parks nose-to-nose with my vehicle.

"Bad news," she hollers, climbing out.

"There are no spare keys?"

She shakes her head. "Unbelievable, huh?"

"You mean to say that Beth gave *me* her only set of keys?"

"Yep. She says a maintenance person lost the other set some time back, and they've never replaced them."

"Oh, jeez." I mutter, feeling horrible, but also irritated. "Well, this is weird then because we've used this set of keys all week. Why would one be missing?"

"Well, it's here somewhere. Are you sure you tried each one."

"I have, but you're more than welcome to give it a go."

She takes the keyring from me and repeats exactly what I've already done several times. The storage unit key was missing.

She gets on the phone with Beth and explains. By the time she hangs up, I've scoured through my 4Runner for the third time. This time, I let Shadow out since it's taking longer than I expected.

"They're sending someone to cut the lock and bring us a new one."

"I'm so sorry. This doesn't make sense. I'd never remove an individual key from a keyring."

"Maybe Greg did—at home?"

"But—why? And the keyring has been in my purse all along."

Soon enough, a truck pulls in behind mine, and a

young man steps out. "Beth Coggins sent me from the community center," he states, grabbing a large device from behind his seat.

We show him which unit it is, and he cuts off the lock within a second.

"I've got a new one for you," I follow him to his truck where he hands me the lock and key.

Hearing Willow's grunts, and then the metal clanging as she lifts the garage-style door, all that seemed normal. Her scream stops me in my tracks.

CHAPTER SEVEN

Both the young maintenance worker and I bolt to Willow's side. Neither of us ask what's wrong; it's clear. The large crate we had stored days prior lies ripped apart, its wood scattered everywhere. Willow's face pales. In stunned silence, she points to where the high-value artifact had been.

"It's gone!" she cries out.

"How?"

The maintenance guy appears unaffected, but antsy. "Anything else I can do? I gotta get back."

I send him on his way. Willow is in shock, so I make the phone call to Beth to explain our latest finding. Before long, all the community center personnel and some law enforcement join us.

"Libby! What happened? What did you do with the key?"

"I, uh…"

"Ma'am, can you come over here for a moment?" An officer calls Beth over, and I stand still, trying to process who could have broken into the storage unit.

I nudge Willow. "Does she think I have something to do with this?"

She shrugs and walks off, joining Beth. I can see Willow pointing in one direction and then another, leaving me questioning whether other items might be missing. Another officer walks up, breaking my concentration.

"Ma'am, are you Libby Madsen?"

I nod. "Yes, I am."

"Can you follow me, please?"

Holding onto Shadow's leash, I guide her and we follow the man over to his cruiser. He asks me several benign questions—to spell my name, what's my age, and what's my address. I answer, and then he asks what I was doing at the storage unit. Explaining everything from the time I started volunteer work for the community center, I try to be as thorough as I can. When it comes to the keys, I simply state what I know for sure. They've been in my possession for several days, and we've come and gone from the storage facility many times.

"Who are the 'we'? Please give me those names."

"Uh, Willow Springs," he glances at me as though I were joking. "No, really. Her name is Willow Springs. She's over there with Beth Coggins inside the unit right now."

"Who else, ma'am? You indicated there were multiple people going in and out."

"Oh, yes. Volunteer workers—um, let's see, I'm not

sure how many I know by name. There was a Crystal."

"Last names?"

I shook my head. "I don't know. Beth would, though."

"Who else?"

"Well, Beth. She came over a time or two. Then there were some teenage boys who helped us lift stuff. I never caught their names."

"And you never handed over the keys to any of these people?"

I struggle to remember. "No, I never directly handed the keys over to anyone. I swear each time we came here, I slid the keyring into my pocket or back inside my purse after unlocking the unit." Pulling it from my jeans pocket, I showed the officer the keyring. "See, I have the keyring right here. The problem is that *one key* is missing."

"What do these other keys open?"

"I have no idea. Again, Beth would know."

After a few more questions where I restate what I'd already answered, he walks back to the storage space.

Beth is beside herself. "This was our one hot ticket item for the fundraiser. Without it, we'll never hit our goals."

"I'm so sorry, Beth. Someone must have stolen the key from the keyring. I can't tell you much more than that." I gently hand the keyring back to her, which includes the new key for the new lock, already hung in place.

Her demeanor turns unfriendly, and I'm unsure whether it's directed toward me or the stress of the situation. When Beth turns and walks away saying nothing else, I feel deflated.

"Willow?" I turn to my friend for assurance.

She reaches out, touching my arm. "She'll be okay. I'm sure she's got a lot on her plate right now."

My phone pings, and I see it's a text from Greg. Somehow, he already knows of the situation—my guess is through Taz. I simply reply that I'll fill him in over dinner this evening.

"So, what now?" I ask Willow.

"Well, it's lunchtime. Let's go grab a sandwich, then we'll check in with Beth and see what she'd like help with next."

Grateful for my new friend's calmness, I follow her lead and soon find myself relaxing. While enjoying our sandwiches, we walk through each step we'd taken unloading items into the storage unit, and neither of us figures out how the key was lost. I feel so responsible.

Over soup for dinner, Greg and I sit out on the patio enjoying the cool evening breeze. Shadow parks herself under my chair, hoping for some bites to fall to the floor.

"I keep going over everything and can't figure out how that key got out of my custody," I say between bites.

"Libby, I'm sure it wasn't your fault."

"Well, the key *is* missing, and someone had to use it to get that lock opened."

"You're sure?"

"Yes! It was the only key, apparently. When we arrived today, the lock was definitely secure. I couldn't get in— that's what took so long."

"Isn't it strange that a thief would take the time to lock it back up?"

"Yeah," my voice softens as I also remember the destruction I saw once we got inside. "I suppose maybe it was meant to stall us?"

He looks confused.

"Meaning, if everything looked fine from the outside, maybe we wouldn't notice for several days. We don't really know when the theft happened."

He shrugs.

"Anyone involved with the volunteer work would know that we were in and out of there multiple times—it was only a matter of time before we'd discover it."

"Unless they thought the work was done?"

"But the fundraiser is only days away … of course, we'd notice by the time the weekend came around. I mean, we have to transfer some of those items back to the community center by Friday."

"True. Any theories?"

"None."

"Hey, on a different subject—how did the massage space work out for you? Apparently, Willow looked impressed."

"Oh, it worked perfectly. And I have already booked several more appointments—and all from the volunteer work. I haven't actually received any referrals from the Mesa location yet."

"Cool—word of mouth is the best referral."

Despite our lovely dinner, I still ruminate on the day's events once I'm lying in bed. I feel responsible for the valuable sculpture going missing, and there's not much to change that. By the time I feel myself drifting off to sleep, I promise myself I'll find the culprit.

The next morning, I wake up to a dreary, rainy morning. I stretch, peeking open one eye, and realizing

Greg has already left for work. Rolling my head in the other direction, I spy Shadow tucked into a tight ball inside her kennel across the room. With the dim, overcast lighting, and the soft patter of rain against the roof, even Shadow isn't eager to wake.

I quietly move my legs off the side of the bed and tiptoe to the bathroom to find my robe. A shiver catches me—much colder than yesterday. When I come back through the bedroom, Shadow's ears perk up, her head tilting sideways. As I unlatch and open her door, she bounces up and starts wiggling around.

"C'mon, sweet girl, let's go find some breakfast." She tears off down the hallway and meets me in the kitchen.

On the countertop, I find a note from Greg. It read: "Both of you girls were sleeping so soundly, I didn't want to wake you. Call me when you are up." I set the slip of paper back down, and pop a K-cup into the Keurig. Coffee first, I decide.

Walking over to the back doors, Shadow and I look out at the drizzle, dreading what comes next.

"Let's get this over with," I tell the black Labrador, whose eyes never leave mine. I slip on the boots I keep near the back door.

She bounds outside and turns back to make sure I am following her out into the rain. I step off the patio stairs, but take my time, hoping she'll be done with her business by the time I catch up to her. No such luck.

I watch Shadow head straight for the guest house. Picking up the pace, not wanting her to venture much farther than that, I hear her bark. My heart plummets at seeing the door to the guest house swing open. Shadow, and her muddy paws, barrel on in, barking her head off.

How the …?

I run, holding my robe closed as I do. When I begin up the steps, the door opens wider, and I freeze in place, seeing the mammoth mountain man standing there.

My hand flies to my mouth, then settles on my chest, fully aware of how little clothing I have on underneath my robe. "Ted, what are you doing here?"

The gentle giant flushes. "Greg didn't warn you?"

I shake my head. Drips of water fly off the ends of my now-soaked hair.

"Sorry, Libby. There were a few things I needed to finish up …" He points inside. "And I'm on my way to another job, so it had to be early. I didn't mean to frighten you."

I step onto the decking and call for Shadow. She comes right away, letting out a woof while still looking warily at the oversized man. Another bark, then Ted excuses himself, apologizing again. I watch him cross the acreage and slide into the cab of his work truck. With another wave, he drives off.

We step into the guest house, and I glance around, but I'm not exactly sure why. Feeling unsettled, nonetheless. Shadow sniffs all around the perimeter, not missing a spot. With another pass through the house, I shrug and call Shadow out through the front door. We cross the yard quickly, dodging the pouring rain. Opening the back door, I smell the coffee I had brewed.

My phone rings, and I grab it from the counter.

"Hello," I huffed.

"Libby. It's Beth."

"Oh, hi! Sorry, trying to catch my wet dog. I wasn't expecting rain."

"Listen, Libby … we have an issue. Are you able to meet me at the center?"

"Sure. When?"

"As soon as you can get here."

"Uh, okay. Let me feed my pup and get dressed. I'm on my way."

Twenty minutes later, I pulled out onto the highway heading toward the community center. My heart flutters, full of nerves. *Was I in for a scolding?* Worse—surely the police would investigate. *Would they really try to pin that theft on me?*

A long horn honk startles me. I look in my rearview mirror to see a large dark truck with the driver gesturing impatiently. A glance down and my odometer shows I'm doing the 40-mile-per-hour speed limit. *What is his hurry?*

Keeping my eyes on the road, I grip the steering wheel and ignore his insistent horn. I know the two-lane road narrows up ahead, and a steady stream of traffic is coming from the opposite direction, not to mention the downpour. My eyes glance between all the mirrors again. The truck was dangerously close to my bumper; any slowing on my part would cause a collision. *What is he doing?* I feel sweat building along my brow. My knuckles grip the steering wheel tight as we approach the curve in the road.

I cringe, gasping as the truck revs up and hurtles around me, narrowly missing a sedan coming toward us. All I hear are horns honking, then I see a sedan hydroplane and nearly lose control as I brake, watching the black Dodge Ram speed out of sight. Looking around to find that sedan, I see they pulled over to the side of the road. I wait for a clearing, then turn around and drive up behind them, turning on my hazard lights.

After letting several cars pass, I carefully exit and walk up to the passenger door of the Kia. A visibly shaken woman opens the window.

"Are you okay?" I ask, looking at her two kids in car seats in the back.

"That man nearly killed all of us!" she exclaims, her voice quivering. "But yes, we're fine."

"Do you live around here?" I ask her.

"Yes, just up the road."

"Did you recognize that truck—know who it might be?"

"I couldn't see well; it all happened so fast. I'm not sure. More than likely, it's a city dweller. They drive like animals up here in the hills all summer."

"Well, you get home safely. Happy to see that you're okay." I leave them and get back in my car.

Beth was waiting inside the doorway. "Where have you been?"

"Sorry, nearly got run off the road—"

She interjects, "We've got a big problem!"

"Okay. How can I help?" I look around at all the busy volunteers, but no one was as frantic as Beth. "If this is about…"

"You have no idea what I've been through in the past twenty-four hours! All this rain overnight has caused huge delays. There's *no way* we'll be ready for the weekend fundraiser!"

I follow her when she turns abruptly and heads into a small storage space. Stopping short of going inside, I see immediately what the issue is. There's at least half an inch of standing water and several soggy cardboard boxes filled with donations.

"Over here," she directs me. "You won't get as wet. It seems to pool at that end."

I tiptoe carefully to the other end of the room.

"We've been removing the contents and getting them to the tables set up out there. The first few boxes we tried picking up broke apart and we made things worse."

Following her lead, I load my arms with stuffed animals, gift baskets wrapped in cellophane, and boxes that hold fundraiser t-shirts. Jose is at the closest table and meets me with open arms.

"Here, we'll start an assembly line," he says to me, grabbing the items from my arms. He turns his head. "Carrie, can you help us?" A young lady comes running to our aid.

Beth hands me more items, and I run them over to Jose and Carrie, who sort through and put them in the right places. That's when I notice there's a table designated for wet items. A huge fan has been set up to blow air across the goods. Another volunteer hung up wet t-shirts on a rack with another fan air drying them.

"You weren't kidding, Beth. This is awful."

"I'm afraid we've probably lost a third of the donations to water damage. Of course we'll try to salvage them, but you should see the paintings we've already had to scrap."

"How did this happen? Roof damage?"

She shakes her head. "The director of the community center said that door over there was wide open when he arrived this morning. We're just lucky the water stayed contained in the storage area and didn't flood the entire building. Could you even imagine?"

I nod slowly, letting the implication of sabotage sink in. Of course, I don't know that for a fact, but it's my gut feeling. Before I can say anything else, the director himself walks up.

"Mr. Erickson, we're nearly done here," Beth greets him and introduces us. When he hears my name, his eyebrows perk up.

"Ah, Libby. Just the one I need to talk to."

My stomach somersaults as I shake his hand, and realize I can't avoid the subject of the offsite storage unit theft.

He clears his throat. "Can you follow me?" He doesn't wait for a response but turns on his heels, and I scramble to keep up with him.

"Is this about that theft, Mr. Erickson?"

"Sure is." He holds his arm out when we come to a hallway. "This way."

"I've been wracking my brain, trying to figure out what could have happened. There was another volunteer—a teen. Maybe there's been a prank…"

"Save it for the deputies."

I gulp audibly, and my stomach lurches.

CHAPTER EIGHT

The handsome young man of average height and cowboy charm turns around and gives me a warm smile. "You must be Libby Madsen?"

I hold my hand out to shake his. "I am."

"I'm Officer Chesky from the Show Low Police Department—we help the Navajo Sheriff's Department occasionally. It's nice to meet you. Please have a seat."

I pull out one of the plastic folding chairs in a room that appears to be set up to serve large group meals. As I lower myself into the seat, I ask, "Do I need a lawyer?"

"Did you do something wrong?" His large brown eyes sparkle with kindness.

"No. I don't think so."

"Then we should be okay. I just need some information,

and I'm sure you will be most helpful."

Mr. Erickson lingers in the doorway. "Will I be needed for this inter … I mean, uh, conversation?"

Officer Chesky twists around in his seat and excuses the director, then turns back to me. "Now, I understand from your initial statement that you had a key to the community center's offsite storage. Is that correct?"

"Yes, it is."

"Can you tell me a little bit about how you came into possession of the key? How long have you volunteered at the center?"

I explain everything. He takes copious notes and only slows when I mention the younger volunteers who helped us that day.

"Do you have their names?"

"Uh…" I close my eyes trying to remember what the high schoolers even looked like. "I'm not certain I ever caught their names."

"Beth only mentioned you and Willow Springs being there. We've talked to Willow—she didn't mention anyone else either."

Confused as ever, I take another minute to search my memory. "Certainly, Beth will know. Maybe she forgot to mention it when you talked to her, but let's call her in and ask. I think she said they were from the local high school football team."

He gives his partner, who I only notice for the first time standing in the room's corner, a head nod, and the woman presumably goes looking for Beth. After what feels like an eternity, with Officer Chesky lobbing questions about the timing of my volunteer work, what specifically I'd worked on, and with whom, finally the female officer returns. She whispers something confidentially in his ear.

"Well, it looks like we have to wrap up for today, but here's my card. If anything else comes to mind, call me. And, Ms. Madsen, don't leave town." He stands, and they walk out, leaving me wondering what happened to the idea of bringing Beth into the conversation.

When I walk down the hall and back into the main social area, I see volunteers everywhere, but no Beth. I poke my head into the small storage space; it's empty, and Beth isn't in there either. I turn to scan the room—no Director Erickson, no Beth, or Willow. In fact, there's no one I recognize, so I step out the front doors. No success there either, so I decide to make myself useful by seeing where I can help. Hours pass by while I help a group of ladies separate donated goods.

My phone chimes, and I pull it from my pocket.

"Willow! I've been wondering where…"

"Libby, come to the parking lot—quick!"

I turn to see that most of the ladies I've been working with have scattered. Guess it's lunchtime. I make my way to the front door. As soon as I step out, a Chevy Traverse skids to a halt. Willow rolls down the window, and all I see is a lady with dark sunglasses resting on her thin, long nose. Her profile reveals pointed features, but I don't recognize her, and she looks straight ahead.

Willow leans in front of the frail figure, who never turns to look in my direction. "Hurry, get in the backseat, Libby!"

I open the back door and climb in quickly, almost afraid she'll speed off before I get my whole body inside. "What's going on? What's the hurry?"

"We need to beat the lunch crowd over at The Mill. Oh, and this is my sister, Joanne."

"Hi Joanne! I hope you had an enjoyable journey here. From Mississippi, right?"

She gives me a slight nod from the driver's seat, wistfully waving a hand, but doesn't speak.

"You scared me, Willow … I thought something else had happened."

"What do you mean?"

"You sounded frantic about me getting into the car and all. Maybe it's me—this morning has been…"

"What happened this morning?"

"Nearly got run off the road to start out. Then, just dealing with Beth's frustration with the flooded items. Next, I had an interesting conversation with Officer Chesky."

Willow let out a little squeal. "Oh, he's a cute one, isn't he?"

I chuckle. *Only Willow.*

Willow's eyes find mine when she turns toward the backseat. "Wait, what *flooded items*?"

"The center's storage area flooded—and by the time I got out of my interview, I couldn't find Beth. They finished getting everything out of that closet, but I'm pretty sure they lost more donations."

"What did Chesky want?"

"Oh, more details about losing that key. Hey, what were the names of those volunteers that helped us lug that sculpture thing?"

"Uh, Kevin … was one of them. I'm not sure I caught the others' names."

We pull into the dirt parking lot of The Mill. Willow wasn't kidding … there's already a line to get inside. She turns to her sister, who remains quiet, staring out the front window. "This is going to be a real treat—you wait."

On our way in, I text Greg, asking whether he's going to stop by home for lunch. Thankfully, he's already there, and Shadow is helping him around the property. I let him know I'd be home after lunch.

"So, Joanne … how long will you be in town?"

Willow cuts in before her sister can answer. "All summer."

Joanne winces, then quietly answers in a soft drawl. "We'll see about that. At least a couple of weeks. *Maybe* I'll be here longer."

"And where are you from in Mississippi?"

She shrugs, a strand of her jet-black hair falling over her right eye. "You probably haven't heard of it. Tunica."

Willow jumps in, explaining that Joanne lost her husband recently. I wonder if that explains the sister's introverted demeanor and presume depression might have its ugly hold on her. She seems awfully withdrawn. Regardless, I also notice immediately that Willow apparently feels it's her place to speak for her younger sister.

Soon enough, a perky, youthful hostess leads us inside the large industrial-style interior, featuring farm-style table settings and a long bar down the center of the room. As I look around the establishment, I imagine the venue hosts nightly live music—there's a small stage and roomy dance floor at the far end of the room.

We each take our seats, order beverages, and peruse a multi-page menu. The restaurant specializes in barbeque, but I'm amazed by the wide selection of options— everything from a full range of sandwiches and soups to home-style meals and a whole page of unique appetizers. We each order a sandwich—I decide on the pulled pork loaded with herb-infused coleslaw. From the moment the hostess walks away, Joanne and I don't have to worry about keeping the conversation going—Willow takes care of that. She chatters on about various subjects, including local gossip, the fundraiser, and even the massage she received from me.

"Jo, you really should try it…"

"I could see what the schedule looks like and maybe get you in tomorrow, if you're interested?" I offer, digging through my purse for my phone.

She squirms in her seat. "Um. I don't…"

"Oh, you just have to try this Shitsu…" Willow's words trail off.

"Ashiatsu," I mutter, scrolling through my scheduling app. "Yep, I'm free tomorrow afternoon if that sounds good."

Willow quickly inserts, "Book it. My treat."

Joanne's mouth twists awkwardly, but before she says anything, Willow changes the subject. I make a mental note to privately ask her sister later—this feels completely forced by Willow.

The sandwiches are placed in front of us, and our conversation slows as we begin devouring our food. It only takes one bite of their specialty sandwich for me to decide that Greg and I need to come here for dinner.

"Seeing anyone, sis?" Willow asks between bites.

Joanne's shoulders shrink forward, setting down the forkful of potato salad she was about to eat. "I'm married."

"Are you? Seems like he's gone, and it's time for you to get back out there. You know, you're not getting any younger."

I feel myself blush for her. Clearly, Joanne is uncomfortable, but Willow doesn't notice, or care, about any of that—she keeps on probing her sister for information throughout our meal.

By the time we finish and before the server brings us our bill, Willow excuses herself for the restroom.

"I'm sorry," I start, reaching a hand out to Joanne. "It must be uncomfortable being asked so many questions in front of a complete stranger."

Her eyes perk up and meet mine. "It's not that. You seem nice."

"Seriously, if you'd like to schedule a massage, I'd be happy to do so. However, please don't do it under duress."

"I'd like to try it." Her eyes dart in the direction her sister had gone. "Does she have to come?"

"No, absolutely not." I pick up my phone, pulling up the app again. "Think you'd be able to do it at two? Day after tomorrow?"

She nods, and I type in the details quickly. "I'll make a call over to the community center and make sure they schedule Willow for volunteer work that afternoon."

Joanne smiles broadly and then asks me how my meal was. We are sharing those thoughts when Willow rejoins us.

"Ah, see. I knew you'd two make fast friends."

I give Joanne a little wink and then we all leave, headed back to the community center.

CHAPTER NINE

I hear the front door close and smile, knowing Greg is home. Shadow runs to greet him, and I hear her paws against the wood floors following him down the hallway toward the bedroom. I keep chopping vegetables as a contented smile spreads across my face.

Fifteen minutes later, I have the veggies steaming and am about to put the seasoned salmon into the air fryer when he sneaks up behind me and snakes his arms around my midsection, startling me. He nuzzles my neck, and I turn around for the kiss. A drop from his newly washed hair lands on my forehead and trails down my face.

"You smell so nice," I mumble, as he reluctantly lets me get back to the salmon. Shadow also nuzzles her way between us; he kneels down and gives her plenty of love, too. "I was surprised to come home to an empty house. But then saw the text you sent about being called in for work. Everything okay?"

His exhale says it all. "Oh, yeah … but let me tell you, after I'd already finished the work around here, I really hadn't planned on doing more physical labor today. But they needed my help—two guys called in sick." He turns to open the fridge and pulls out an ice-cold beer. "Ah well. We made great progress this afternoon—still, it'll take the entire summer to finish." Popping off the cap with a bottle opener, he asks me, "How about your day? All ready for the fundraiser this weekend?"

I fill him in, purposely avoiding the part where a pickup nearly ran me off the road. He's surprised to hear about the damage to the community center from the overnight rain.

"Seems to me like an inside job," he comments.

Questioningly, I glance over at him. "A rain storm?"

He shrugs. "No, the door being left open. It seems you'd have to be *inside* the community center to do that, right? So, someone with the keys to the center came in, and maybe they left a door open to steal more stuff? Only the rain came and wrecked their plans."

Shadow lets out a funny sound, as though she's commenting on our conversation. We both smile, wondering if she was.

I think about his theory as I pull out the automatic bottle opener and use it on a fresh bottle of Cabernet Sauvignon. *Is that how the rain got inside—through an outside door?* I struggle to remember.

"I'm just trying to figure out the motive, though. Everyone involved has put in so much time and effort on this event, I can't imagine who'd want to sabotage it.

I mean, we all want the firefighters to make as much as possible during the silent auction. Why would an insider with the fundraiser impede that?"

Woof!

I look down at Shadow. "Really? You think it's someone on the inside, sweet girl?"

Woof!

"Have you taken her outside recently?"

"Oh! That's probably it," I chuckle.

He calls her to the back door, and I watch them head out across the property. Taking a sip of my wine, I count my blessings again—a wonderful man, a beautiful place in the cool mountains for the summer, and I have already met several nice people. My mind goes back to Joanne. She's an interesting one. Then again, so is her sister.

The buzzing air fryer diverts my attention back to finishing up our meal.

When the back door opens, I have each plate loaded with the salmon and a colorful array of roasted vegetables. I pour myself a little more wine.

"Can I get you another beer?"

"I'll have a glass of wine, please."

Once settled at the table, I tell him all about lunch with the ladies. He doesn't understand my concern about the sisters' relationship. All siblings have their thing. And he's not wrong there—I only have to look as far as the relationship with my sister. I love her immensely, but I can't really stand being around her for too long. Point made.

"So, you should be fairly close to being done with the weekend preparations, right?"

"I think so. Although it seems as though Beth is super stressed, and every time I think we've priced the last of the stuff, well, there's more. So, who really knows? I'm having fun though."

"Great. And you have another massage booked—any more leads from the office?"

"Yes, I'm working on Joanne tomorrow. Other leads… no, not really. Lexi seems disappointed. Well, I am too, really. I'm hoping it will pick up soon."

We kick around a few more ideas about who could be stealing from the community center, but nothing really sticks out to me as revelations I can take to the police.

Once we finish cleaning up after dinner, we snuggle up on the sofa and find an action-adventure movie on Netflix. Both of us fall asleep before the movie ends.

* * *

When the bright sunbeam crosses my face in the morning, I reach out and feel that Greg has already left. I stretch out, listening to see if I can hear Shadow stirring yet. All is quiet in the house, so I let my eyes close again.

The next time I open my eyes, I realize another hour has passed. I quickly sit up and check my phone. No missed messages, but I see it's already nine o'clock, and I can't remember the last time I'd slept in that late.

Hurrying about, I get my workout clothes on, lace up my trainers, and get Shadow from her little house. We step out into the sunshine and set off on a jog. The mountain air was warming, but still had a nice crispness to it. We round the end of the street and keep running—Shadow darting in front of me several times, chasing some scent. By the time we make it back to the house, I am more than ready for coffee. My phone vibrates in my pocket as I struggle to unlock the door and maintain a hold on Shadow's leash.

"Hi Beth," I answer.

"Libby, what did you tell Officer Chesky yesterday?"

"Um, why?"

"They've called in all the volunteers now for questioning."

Not understanding the problem, I let the silence hang in the air for a second.

Beth sighs. "Sorry. That came out as an accusation. I meant only that he seems to think it's an inside job."

"Maybe it is? I certainly didn't tell him that, but isn't it possible? Shouldn't he be looking at all angles?"

I hear what sounds like paperwork shuffling around. "Of course. Of course."

"What's on the schedule for today? Do you need me to come in?"

"No, not today. Willow and Joanne are already here, and we had a good turnout. I think we're nearly ready, even with the stolen donations."

"Okay, I'll stop by later to get my schedule and assignments for the big weekend—two more days!"

"I should have them ready before five this evening—" she hesitates. "Actually, maybe tomorrow morning. Come by then."

Relief washes over me as I realize I have an entire day to myself without volunteer work. I pour myself a mug of coffee, and Shadow follows me outside: it's time to work on the new guest house.

* * *

Later that evening, I convince Greg to go to The Mill

for dinner. As suspected, it's in full swing, with country western dancing and a live band. At the bar, we have a drink while waiting to be seated.

"Hey, Greg! Good to see you, man!" A redheaded guy with a long beard comes up and shakes his hand.

When he and his date continue to their table, I turn to my fiancé. "Everyone knows you in this town."

"Well, I wouldn't say *everyone*, but it's a very small town so…" he trails off as Taz comes up and slaps his back.

"Dude, finally bringing the lady out," she teases, winking at me.

I look around for her partner but don't see Beth. "Good to see you again, Taz."

"And you, Libby. Beth is still working up the schedules and all for the big weekend. I'm used to it. I rarely get her attention during fundraiser events—she's a mighty focused woman." She takes another long pull on her beer. "Gonna get out there and dance, y'all?"

We both chuckle. Taz's attention is distracted by another friend who pulls her out onto the dance floor.

"Do you line dance?" Greg asks me.

"I mean, I have tried it, but I'm not all that good."

"Later. I'll show you a few tricks."

The server calls our name, and we follow her to the booth. Thankfully, it's on the opposite side from the band.

"I used to love to dance," Greg reminisces. "It's been a while though. You know, they have lessons here too, so we could brush up on our skills. Maybe this summer and before the wedding?"

I perk up. A man who wants to take dance lessons? Okay!

We place our food orders and also order more beer.

When we look over to the dance floor, we see Taz twirling her friend around on the dance floor, and everyone whooping it up. Before our barbecue platters arrive at the table, a skirmish near the bar catches everyone's attention.

Greg bolts over there. It was his friend, Ted. Greg and a few other guys pull him away, leading the burly man outside. I see Taz offering her hand, helping a man up from the ground, wiping blood from his mouth. He picks up his cowboy hat and takes a seat at the bar, and she heads in my direction.

"What was that about?" I ask Taz.

She shrugs. "You never know with Ted these days."

"Oh? How so?"

"I'm not sure how much I should say. I certainly don't need to get on his bad side."

We both look over at the dance floor again, and everyone has resumed line dancing, the quarrel already a distant memory. I glance toward the front door, wondering where Greg is and praying he won't get involved.

"Hey, this is one of my favorites," Taz points to the dance floor. "Join me!" She reaches out for my hand. I lift my wineglass, shaking my head.

"I'll wait for Greg—any idea where they went? Our food should be here shortly."

She shakes her head, turns, and heads over to her group.

Not long after, I see Greg making his way through the crowd. The grimace on his face tells me he isn't thrilled, but he says nothing as he flops down into his seat.

The server shows up with our food, and the platter set in front of us has an enormous serving of brisket and chicken. Then come the side dishes, dinner rolls, green chile macaroni and cheese, herb-infused coleslaw, and some extra barbecue sauce. We help ourselves, dishing up each of the selections onto our plates.

"Does he often get into fights?"

Greg lets out a sigh as he glances around the room. "Something's going on with him, but I can't make out what. That—" he points in the direction where the earlier fight happened, "is completely out of character for Ted. I've never seen him raise his voice, much less clock someone in the jaw." He takes a swig of his beer, and when he sets it back down on the table, he leans forward. "He's not said much to me. Any rumors at the community center?"

"Taz insinuated he's going through something. She wouldn't say what, but I was hoping maybe he confided in you out there."

He slowly shakes his head and takes another bite.

"Did he go home?"

"I hope so. The bartender asked him to go cool down."

After we box up the leftovers, we share one of their skillet-baked brookies—brownie and oatmeal cookie— topped with a scoop of vanilla bean ice cream. Before I can finish my share, my phone vibrates in my pocket. It's Joanne, confirming the two o'clock appointment for the next day. Greg must have seen the smile on my face as I replaced the phone in my pocket.

"Whatcha up to?" he grinned.

"Oh, I mentioned how I met Willow's sister, Joanne. For some reason, she doesn't want Willow to know she booked the massage. So, I figured a way to get Willow doing volunteer work so Joanne could sneak over and get a massage."

Greg gives me that skeptical look guys give when they

can't figure out women.

"Yeah, I don't know what it was all about, but she's strange around her sister. I mean, Willow can be quite overpowering, I guess. Joanne seems subdued. Well, opposites, I suppose."

"And how is the fundraising work going?"

"Well, I still feel as though all eyes have been on me since losing that key."

"Certainly, they don't think that you had anything to do with it."

I nod. "I do feel responsible, even though I've done nothing wrong."

He reaches across the table, giving my hand a gentle squeeze. His kind eyes tell me everything will be okay.

Not long afterward, we pay our bill and head out. Taz tried one more time to get us to dance, but we both prefer an evening alone at home instead.

Glancing around the parking lot on the way to Greg's Tundra, I see a man leaning against the far end of the building. Although the night's shadows deepened, I swear it's the man who'd been hit in the nose earlier.

Once we are safely in the truck, I point him out to Greg. "Wonder why he's still hanging around?"

He starts the truck and swiftly leaves the parking lot. "We don't need to get tied up in Ted's issues."

"So, you do think he's involved in something then?"

"I'm not sure. The Ted I've known has always been a gentle person. But then again, how well do we know anyone?"

The ping I hear coming from my pocket pulls my attention away. It was my sister, Jordan.

"Well, hello there. What's up?"

"Hi Libby, it's Jordan." She still introduces herself even though cell phones show who's calling.

"How are you? How are the kids?"

"Well, Apple and Annie keep pestering me about coming up to see you. I wasn't sure whether you were serious about that? But if you are, what about this weekend? Well, for the next week, actually. Remember, Mom will be on her trip."

I glance over at Greg and wonder how much he'd heard through the earpiece. "Right now, we're on our way home from dinner. Let me get settled back at home and talk to Greg—I'll give you a call back in a little bit. Would that work?"

"Yes, of course. Sorry to interrupt."

I laugh, rolling my eyes. "You're not interrupting anything. Don't worry. I'll call you back in a few." I punch the button to end the call and turn to Greg, reminding him about my mom's trip and Jordan's need for a sitter.

"What do you think of having my nieces up to visit for a while?"

"That'd be fantastic. How long?"

"A week?"

"Sure! Will they help you at the fundraising event?"

"Yeah. I'll talk to Beth and see if we can put them to work." Once home, Greg offers to take Shadow outside while I call my sister back. Within half an hour, we make plans; she'll bring the twins to us. Greg puts a kettle on for tea so we can retire to the comfy sofa in front of a roaring fire.

CHAPTER TEN

The next morning is a flurry of activity—the last day to prepare for the big fundraising event. Beth's in rare form when Shadow and I arrive early with coffee and donuts in hand. She snatches one of the chocolate-glazed from the box and gives a little moan, swallowing her first sip of the vanilla almond latte.

"Thank you, Libby," she says, taking a huge bite from the donut.

"Would this be a good time to mention that I have a couple more volunteers for the weekend?"

Her eyes widen, and her head bobs up and down. "We can always use more help," she mutters as she gulped down the bite of donut.

"They're teenagers—but pretty responsible. It's my

nieces—they're twins!"

"Perfect."

"What can I help with this morning? I just need to be home by lunchtime."

She checks the clipboard that holds her carefully crafted schedule. "I'm putting you in charge of—oh! I don't have you on the schedule today, Libby. That's weird."

My spirit fades.

"Let's see," she grimaces as she flips through the pages. Her phone chimes, and without missing a beat, she looks at the message that pops up. "Hey, can I send you on a little errand?"

"Sure! However I can help."

She rattles off a set of instructions to drive over to an address in Show Low, pick up three boxes, and bring them back to her at the community center. No problem— Shadow and I can easily handle that.

* * *

The thirty-minute drive to Show Low is no problem at all. Finding the address Beth gave me proves to be far more challenging. First, the address isn't actually in the town of Show Low, but I find it on the outskirts of the small town called Pinetop-Lakeside.

Figuring it was an address for a business had me questioning Google Maps the entire way, when it directed me to a location in a mobile home park. All this is to say that I really should ask more questions before launching in to help run errands.

I follow the final turn as directed by Google Maps and slowly proceed down a row of mobile homes that appear unoccupied. I slam on my brakes as a scraggly old dog lumbers out in front of my 4Runner. He sits in the middle of the street, and I honk, staring at him. The black-gray, long-haired mutt simply glares back at me, making no effort to move.

Since Shadow is focused, looking out the left side of the vehicle, I decide to help the dog out of the road. Before I can open the door, though, Shadow lets out a sharp bark, causing me to jump, and bump my head against the headrest. *Ow!*

The old dog pays no attention to us; instead, he sprawls out in the street, with no cares in the world. I turn to see what Shadow is barking at. The only thing in sight is a rusted white and green trailer with an awning that tilts precariously close to falling from the structure. Between the doorway and the front window, I also see the faded black numbers 36 with the number 2 dangling from the house's siding.

I look back at my phone—this is the address! 362 Mitchell Rd.

"Shadow, wait here. I'll be right back." I lower the windows so she has fresh air, and give her the signal one more time for 'stay'.

Carefully opening my car door, I talk sweetly to the dog who has commandeered the road. He barely lifts his head as I walk by him, past the littered front yard, and up the overgrown pathway to the front door.

When I lift my hand to knock, a pungent smell hits me so hard I cover my nose with my shirt, trying not to gag. That's when I notice the door is standing ajar. I push it open wider with my foot and call out, "Hello!"

Something brushes against me, and I scream, jumping

backward and twisting my ankle at the same time. Grabbing for my ankle, I see it's the dog from the road that sauntered into the home. I rap loudly against the door, cautiously step over the threshold, and follow the dog inside.

"Hello! Anyone home? I'm here to…" I abruptly stop, seeing a body prone on the floor. "Oh, no. No, no, no…" I mutter, staring at the bluish hue to his face and extremities.

Swiveling around to bolt, Shadow bounds past me. "Shadow! NO!" I miss her, watching her launch right into the kitchen with the other dog. The older mutt growls, and Shadow backs away barking. "Come here, Shadow!"

I kneel down, seeing there's no hope of reviving this man. He's clearly dead. "Let's get out of here, come on girl…" She does as told, and as soon as we're outside, the older mutt peers out the front door and gives another woof.

I immediately pull out my phone and dial 911. As we wait for the police to arrive, I call Beth.

"What? Mr. Sanchez is dead?" She was breathless, spitting out the words. "But I just got the call for the donation pickup this morning, minutes before you headed over there."

"Beth, he's been dead for a while. The smell…" I decide to spare her the details. "Look, the police are coming up the street. I'll fill you in later. What exactly was I to pick up from him? You know, in case the police ask."

"Some coins."

"Okay, I'll call you back." As I punch the button on my phone, I see three police cruisers coming to a halt and, for the first time, I notice people gathering in the neighborhood. Guess that answers my previous suspicion about whether the mobile home park was vacant. Now, as I glance around, I see glares from everyone; I'm clearly the outsider in their neighborhood.

I snap the leash onto Shadow's collar and hold her tightly to my side as the first two officers approach us.

"Good morning, officer … my name is Libby Madsen. I found Mr. Sanchez on his kitchen floor." My speech flows as fast as my pulse spikes, remembering my arrival at the man's home.

"Ma'am, slow down. Let's take this one step at a time." While Officer Torres pulls out a small notebook from his chest pocket, I watch three others approach the home. "Is there anyone else in the home?"

Good question. "Uh, no. Not that I saw anyway. Honestly, I was only in there for a couple minutes. The smell…" Looking back to the doorway, I notice the officers put masks and gloves on before entering. The youngest of them hangs back until one of his peers pushes him forward. "It's nasty in there."

"How do you know the deceased?" he asks pointedly.

"Well, uh … I don't. You see, it all started this morning when… Um, well, I am volunteering for the Heber…"

"Spare me the storytelling. How do you know this homeowner?"

"I don't. I was sent on an errand to pick up some coins from him."

"Coins?"

"Well, yes, part of the story you don't want me to tell."

He clears his throat. "Ms. Madsen, are these valuable coins?"

"I really don't know."

Our heads whip around when an officer calls out. "Officer Torres, you are going to want to see this!"

"Stay right here, Ms. Madsen." He tucks the notepad

back into his pocket, turns on his heel, and rushes up to the house.

Petting Shadow's head, I glance around at all the prying eyes staring at us. Only one lady, with short black hair and gray streaks through it, gives a little smile. When I respond in kind, she shuffles over to me.

"Is Marty okay?" she whispers. "Are you the daughter he's always talking about?"

I shake my head, not knowing how much to divulge. "No, I'm not his daughter. I came by to pick something up from him."

"Oh." Her eyes widen, and she turns to watch the activity through the front door.

"Do you know Mr. Sanchez well?"

"Mr. Sanchez?"

"Yeah," I point to his home.

"I don't know a Mr. Sanchez. That's Marty Spiegel's home."

Now more confused than ever, I have a sinking feeling. I stand, listening to the neighbor lady's story of how she'd met Marty and all the kind favors he'd done for her over the years. How all the neighbors always stepped up to help one another—it was a tight-knit community.

I point out the dog who's again napping in the street. "Is that his dog?"

"Oh, no. That's Mr. Bandolini's—four doors down. His name is Tiger."

"I think Tiger purposefully stopped me while I was driving down the road. Maybe to come help Mr. Sanch ... I mean, Mr. Spiegel? It just so happened it was also the address I was looking for."

Her mouth makes another *ohhhh* gesture, but no

words come out. When she notices the cop heading in our direction, she hurries off to the gathering crowd without another word.

No sooner is the nice little old lady back with the group when another one of them shouts out, "Liar!" I turn around to see a lady shaking her fist at me.

Shock roots me in place. I feel someone touch my arm. I whirl around to face Officer Torres. "Ms. Madsen, who did you say you came to visit at this house?"

Still rattled by the woman's outburst, I stammer. "Uh, well … I was told I was meeting Mr. Sanchez. However, I just learned from the nice lady over there—not the one yelling at me—that the house belongs to a Marty Spiegel."

He twisted to look where I pointed, then shook his head. "Yes. But the man inside is neither of those you've mentioned."

"Who is it?"

"We're unsure. But the deceased has an ID in his pocket. It's definitely neither of those names, and the picture looks nothing like the John Doe."

I shrug, not understanding what's happening.

"We're going to need you to follow us to the station so we can get an official statement from you. This man has stab wounds, so this is officially a crime scene now."

My stomach turns over. I clear my throat, trying to will myself not to be sick. I don't want to be involved in any investigation. And I need to get back home; I have work to do, I remember, as I sneak a peek at my watch.

"Got somewhere to be?" Officer Torres remarks.

"Well, yes. I'm supposed to get back to the community center in Heber. And then back to my full-time job just after lunchtime. Will this take long?"

"As long as it takes for you to tell your story."

Internally I groan, wanting to scream to him that I *had* tried telling my story and he wouldn't let me.

"Anywhere you can drop off your dog?"

"No, unless I'm allowed to go back to Heber first."

He nods. "Alright. You can bring him along, I guess."

"Her," I quietly state as I make my way to my vehicle. Turning back to the officer, "Am I following you?"

He nods, then shouts something to another officer. As I get my vehicle turned around on the narrow street, I notice an officer talking with the neighbors. And as we pull out onto the main street outside the mobile home park, I see the coroner's van signaling to turn in.

CHAPTER ELEVEN

Following a police cruiser through the center of Pinetop-Lakeside is a surreal experience—especially with a retriever panting in the back seat like we're on the way to a dog park, not a police interrogation.

Shadow at least, seems content. Her tail thumps on the seat as she watches the flashing blue lights up ahead, blissfully unaware that the world has dropped out from under my feet. I grip the steering wheel, trying not to hyperventilate. This morning, I was only supposed to pick up some coins. What a simple task. Now, there's a dead man, a cop telling me I need to give an "official statement," and a neighbor lady calling me a liar in front of God and everyone. What the hell just happened?

I force myself to take a breath, in through the nose,

out through the mouth. I've coached dozens of clients, but in this moment, my own advice is as useful as a screen door on a submarine. My phone is still on the console, blinking with an unread text. Probably Beth, wondering why I'm not back yet. Or maybe Greg, already sensing the disturbance in the universe.

I can't do this alone. I reach for the phone at a red light and punch in Greg's number with trembling fingers. He answers on the first ring, his voice warm but also distracted. "Hey, Libs."

"Hi," I say, and my voice cracks on the second syllable. "Are you, um, busy?"

I hear him moving, the soft shuffle of boots.

"Just wrangling a broken sprinkler head. You okay?"

"I'm following a police car." There's no gentle way to say it, so I blurt everything out. "To the station. There was—Greg, there was a body. The guy was dead. And the neighbor said the address wasn't even right, and the police think I might have … I don't know what the police think. They're asking me to make an official statement."

There's a heavy pause. In the back, Shadow lets out a soft whine, picking up on my panic. Greg's voice comes back steady, forest-ranger calm. "Okay. Slow down. Are you alright?"

"I'm not hurt," I say, glancing around, seeing the cop still in front of me. "But I'm totally freaked out. They said it's a crime scene. Greg, the guy was *stabbed*." I realize I'm practically yelling.

"Whoa." His breath whistles through the phone. "You found a murdered guy? Back the story up—what are you doing and *where* are you?"

"I was supposed to pick up coins for the fundraiser.

I think there was an address mix-up, well, maybe; I'm not really sure. But—I went where I was told, following Google Maps, and when I went in, the door was open and—" I squeeze my eyes shut for a half second. "He was on the floor. And then the neighbor said I had the wrong house. No, maybe she said the man I was looking for doesn't live there. Oh, I'm so mixed up! But the police said it was the right address, only the man inside wasn't the guy who owned it—he was someone else. And I think the police might think I had something to do with it, or at least, I don't know, that I'm some kind of suspect, but I can't explain why—"

Shadow barks, loud and sharp, like she's had enough of my babbling. Greg's voice becomes soft and careful, the same way he talks to skittish hikers. "Breathe, Libby. Just tell them everything you told me. They just want to get the facts, so only give them facts you are sure about."

"What if they arrest me?" I whisper.

He chuckles, low and gentle. "Then I'll bail you out. But they won't. You've done nothing wrong."

I stare at the passing pine trees, the dappled morning sunlight blurring with my vision. "Will you take care of Shadow if they — I mean, if I have to be in here for a while?"

"Of course."

I glance at the GPS and read off the cross-streets just before turning into the parking lot. We pull into the police station, the cruiser rolling to a stately halt under the battered blue-and-white sign. I park in the visitors' section. My stomach sours and my hands shake again.

Greg sighs. "Call me as soon as you know anything." His voice lowers, like he's giving me a hug through the phone. "Libby, you're going to be fine. Just tell them the truth. Don't let them trip you up. Only facts—and at any time, you can ask for a lawyer. In fact, should I make a few calls?"

It's tempting, but I know he's up to his eyeballs in work. "I'll be fine. And yes, I'll follow your advice. If they back me into a corner, I'll ask to make a call and we'll figure out legal representation then. Hopefully, it won't come to that."

"Exactly. Call me the minute you know anything," he says. "You got this."

"Thanks," I mumble, and hang up before I start ugly-crying. I turn toward the back seat, reaching out to Shadow as she leans into my hand, her body radiating patient optimism. I want to believe it's that simple.

"Okay, girl," I say, unbuckling Shadow's harness from the seat. "Let's see how bad this gets."

I climb out and see the officer waving me inside. The morning is bright, but my mind is clouded with every worst-case scenario I've ever read in a true crime novel. I keep replaying the image of the man on the floor.

The cop at the door gives me a smile that is meant to be comforting, but instead it makes me feel like I'm about to be dissected under a microscope. I take a deep breath and step through the glass doors, Shadow at my side. I don't even know what I'm about to say, but I try to remember Greg's voice: *Just tell the truth. Only the facts.* I hope the truth is enough.

They park me in a lime-green vinyl chair beneath a poster that says: "WE CARE ABOUT YOUR SAFETY," which feels like an elaborate joke. Shadow leans against my knee, still radiating canine calm; the desk sergeant says I can bring her in.

I wait, staring at the ceiling tiles and counting the flickering lights. Across the room, a man in a mechanic's uniform flips through an old *Car and Driver*, ignoring me. I rehearse my story: coins, fundraiser, address, dead body. My hands are still jittery.

"Ms. Madsen?" A female officer in a pressed uniform waves me over. She's got a high ponytail, a perfectly squared jaw, and the kind of arms that say CrossFit and take no prisoners. I grab Shadow's leash and shuffle over to her, praying I won't faint or throw up.

"Let's get your statement," she says, opening a door. "You can bring your dog, so long as she behaves." The way she eyes Shadow tells me she's skeptical.

She leads us into a tiny interrogation room with the air conditioner set to arctic. The table is metal, the chairs scarred from who knows what. There's a glass of water and a legal pad already on my side.

"Officer Rabideau," she says, sliding into the chair across from me. She opens a manila folder and flips to the first page, clicking her pen. "Let's start at the top."

I swallow, glance at Shadow, then look back at the officer. "Should I—um, do I need a lawyer?"

She smiles. "Unless you have something to hide?"

"No."

"Then walk me through your morning."

I tell her about the call from Beth, the errand, the directions. I mention the community center, the silent auction, my volunteer work. My voice goes thin and fluttery as I get to the part about following Google Maps to the address, the open door, the smell. I try to be clinical, but my throat keeps closing up. Shadow rests her chin on my lap as if to say, *keep going.*

Officer Rabideau doesn't interrupt, just scribbles notes. When I'm done, she sits back, tapping her pen on the folder. "Let's go back. This 'Beth'—last name?"

"Coggins," I say, relieved to have an answer. "She runs the community center's volunteer programs."

"And she called you today?"

"She texted me the address after we first met in person at the community center," I say, and fumble for my phone. My hands are trembling as I scroll to the message.

Officer Rabideau holds up her hand. "Let's finish the timeline. You arrived at the address—362 Mitchell Road. What time?"

"Ten, maybe? I left Heber around nine-thirty."

Rabideau just waits, pen poised. "You said the front door was open?"

"Not open, open," I say, "but ajar. I knocked and called out. When nobody answered, I—I realize how bad this sounds. I went in. I thought maybe the guy needed help."

"Why would you think that?"

"I don't know. I used to do a lot of home visits for clients, for elderly people. If a door's open and they're not answering, you worry." My heart's thudding.

"And you found the deceased … where, exactly?"

"In the kitchen. On the floor. The dog—Tiger, the neighbor called him—went inside first. He seemed to know the way. Or maybe he smelled … I mean, he just went straight in."

She writes this down. "Did you touch the body?"

"No! I called 911 right away. I tried to get Shadow out of there, but she followed the other dog. When I saw— when I saw he was blue, I just, I left. I got both dogs outside and waited for the police."

There's a quiet moment as she looks me over, as if she sees actual blood on my hands. "Who was the deceased to you?"

I shake my head. "No one. I've never seen him before in my life."

Officer Rabideau leans forward. "Then why did you have the key to his home?"

My brain stutters. "What? I didn't. The door was unlocked."

She holds up a sheet from her folder. "You said the address was for a Mr. Sanchez. The neighbor says it belongs to a Marty Spiegel."

My mind spirals, remembering how the police are great at catching one off guard. I struggle to remember names. *What did she say about a key?*

I sit up straighter and stare right into her eyes. "I … I don't know. Beth just assigned me the task and texted me the address and said, 'Pick up the coins from Sanchez, 362 Mitchell Road.' That's all I had." I feel my face getting hot. "Look, I know this sounds crazy, but I don't know these people. I just do what Beth asks. I help with fundraisers."

Rabideau makes a show of jotting down every word. "And yet you entered a stranger's home. That's unusual behavior, Ms. Madsen."

"It's not, actually." My voice goes up half an octave. "Volunteers do porch pickups all the time—donations, online orders, even groceries. I figured it was like that."

She gives me a polite, predatory smile. "Except you didn't find coins. You found a corpse."

I stare at my lap, twisting the leash around my finger. Shadow licks my knee, and I nearly start crying.

"Alright." She closes the folder. "Let's bring in my partner. He's got a few follow-ups."

She leaves and in comes a man who looks like every small-town police chief in every TV show—grizzled, mustache, craggy face, probably drinks Folgers from a mug that says #1 Grandpa. He sits across from me, arms folded, looking unimpressed.

"I'm Sergeant Sweeney," he says. "Let's not beat around the bush, Ms. Madsen. We have a dead man and a witness with an odd story. Tell me again why you were at that trailer?"

I repeat the story, word for word, but it sounds even less believable the second time. He interrupts, asking about the fundraiser, about Beth, about why I went inside instead of waiting on the porch. He asks if I ever met Mr. Sanchez, if I ever spoke to him on the phone, if I had any connection at all.

"No," I say, each time, my voice getting smaller.

"Did you touch anything inside?"

"I don't think so." But now I'm not so sure. "Maybe the door? And Shadow was with me, so she might've…"

He raises an eyebrow. "Your dog is a Labrador, right?"

"Retriever," I say, which is technically true, but he waves it off.

"We'll need her prints too," he says, and it's only then that I realize they dusted prints at the scene. I imagine the lab analysis coming back with a big fat match, and for a horrible second, I think maybe they'll try to arrest Shadow. It wouldn't be the first time, actually. But that's impossible, so I take another deep breath.

Sweeney softens, just a little. "We're not accusing you, Ms. Madsen. But you have to see how this looks."

"I do," I say. "But I swear, I only showed up to get a box of coins. That's it."

He sighs, scribbles something, and stands. "Don't leave the state, Ms. Madsen. And if you think of anything else— anyone who might've had access to that address, anyone who stood to gain from this man's death—you call us. Understood?"

I nod, feeling like a third grader who's flunked the test. "Yes, sir."

He leaves me alone in the cold room with Shadow and the glass of water, which I finally sip. When Officer Rabideau returns, she's thawed maybe half a degree.

Officer Rabideau says they're done with me and walks me back to the lobby—"You're free to go," like it's a blessing and not a test.

But I've barely made it five steps across the sticky tiles before a plainclothes detective blocks my path, all stubble and cheap cologne, holding a yellow legal pad like a weapon.

"Ms. Madsen, could we trouble you for just a few more minutes?"

His smile is pure shark. My knees lock, and I say yes even though every cell in my body screams for the exit.

They shepherd Shadow and me to a new room, smaller than the first, and with two battered chairs and a folding table. Detective Stubble introduces himself as Munson, and his partner as Sanders—a no-nonsense woman with red-framed glasses and a sharp, angular voice.

"We just want to clarify a few things," Munson says. "You don't mind, do you?"

I shake my head. I know better than to ask for a lawyer. That makes you look suspicious, doesn't it?

Sanders opens the show: "You said you were picking

up coins. But when our team went through the scene, there was no evidence of a package, envelope, or even a note. What exactly were you expecting to find, Ms. Madsen?"

I replay the moment in my head, over and over, but there's nothing there. Just the address, the memory of Beth's text, and then the horror-show inside. "I don't know," I say, which sounds pathetic. "Beth said to pick up a donation for the fundraiser. That's all I know."

Munson narrows his eyes.

Sanders jots notes, glancing at me like she's catching a lie on every syllable. "According to public records, the owner is Martin Spiegel. But the deceased had identification in his pocket—last name, Blankenship. You ever heard those names before?"

I shake my head again, getting impatient with the repeated questions. "No. Never."

Munson leans in, elbows on the table. "Here's what bothers me, Ms. Madsen: the neighbor across the street says she's never seen you before. She also says Mr. Spiegel is alive and well. So, what brings this Blankenship, a man with no known ties to this neighborhood, into that house?"

"I don't know," I whisper, and I honestly don't.

The room hums with fluorescent light and something darker, like the expectation that I'm about to confess to a homicide. I can't stop my hands from shaking.

Sanders circles back: "You said the dog—Tiger—led you into the trailer. Is that right?"

"Yes."

Munson flips a page on the legal pad. "You sure you weren't in there before, Ms. Madsen?"

"No. Never."

He lets the silence stretch, then says, "Would anyone

else vouch for you? Confirm your timeline?"

"Shadow," I say, and instantly hate myself. "Sorry. No, just me. And maybe Beth—can confirm when I was at the community center in Heber, what time I left, and then I'm sure you can do the math for how long a drive it is. That's all I've got." I scramble for my phone to show them the message, but Sanders lifts her hand.

"We've already seen it." She looks at her printout.

I shrug, helpless. "That's what I got."

They keep repeating the questions, circling the same empty drain. Why didn't I verify the pickup? Was I aware of any prior connection between Beth and the deceased? Did I have any reason to harm this man? Did I know who did?

They test every version of my story, searching for the moment I snap and confess to a motive I don't have. By twelve-thirty, my hands are numb and my head is a hive of self-doubt. I wonder what evidence they have.

When they finally let me go, it's with a warning: "Stay local. Answer your phone. We'll be in touch."

I lead Shadow into the bright hallway, then step outside. My knees almost buckle with relief.

I text Greg: Out. Not arrested. On my way home—Will call later.

As I walk to my car, I catch my reflection in the side window—a pale, wild-eyed woman with damp auburn hair and coffee stains down her sleeve. She looks guilty as hell. *Is that really how I looked to those officers?* I take a breath, rub Shadow's ears, and remember the two o'clock appointment on my calendar.

But something is very wrong. I feel it in the pit of my stomach.

In the car, I text Beth the summarized version of what happened. When she doesn't reply right away, I add: They want to talk to you. Please call me ASAP.

I sit behind the wheel for a long minute, trying to calm my racing heart. Then I check the clock: less than an hour to get home for my two o'clock appointment. I turn the ignition and peel out, scanning the rearview mirror, half-expecting a squad car to follow.

I don't want to be alone, but I also don't want to see anyone. *Maybe I should just cancel the appointment?* No, it will be a good distraction this afternoon. My head pounds from every question they asked me, and a hundred more that I wish I'd thought to ask them.

* * *

The driveway is in full sun, blinding off the hood of Joanne's Traverse as I pull in. She's parked so far from the house it looks deliberate, as if my front porch might bite. I see her behind the windshield, sunglasses on, spine ramrod straight, hands clamped on the wheel at ten and two. I peek in the mirror, combing my hair with my fingers, deciding it's good enough until I get inside.

Shadow whines the second she sees the car, tail thrashing the back seat. "We made it, girl," I say, though I don't believe it. I check the dashboard clock: 1:59 p.m.

Joanne waits until we get out of our vehicle, then she steps lightly onto the gravel, arms folded, lips cracking a smile. There's an awkward half-wave between us, then nothing. I hear the tick of her car cooling as she closes the door. She's wearing athletic leggings and a faded Ole Miss t-shirt, her hair wound tight at the nape of her neck. Her body language says she's ready to sprint, not "here for a spa day."

"Hi," I say, trying to sound cheerful, and my voice comes out brittle. "Sorry I'm late. Got held up in Show Low."

She nods, then glances at the sky, then at her feet. "No problem," she says. "I'm early."

Shadow bounds ahead, loping straight to Joanne's side. Instead of recoiling, Joanne gives her a brisk rub behind each ear. "You're sweet," she says to the dog, but her eyes flick to me, sharp and searching.

I fumble for my keys, drop them, and then usher us across the new lawn. "Come on over—I set up my business in our guest house."

Inside, everything is in order, precisely where I left it, and the scent of spearmint and eucalyptus still hovers.

Joanne lingers in the doorway. "Is this where you do it?"

"Yes," I say, feeling her question land heavier than what she meant. "I have the space set up in the back room. You can leave your shoes here, or—"

She slips them off before I finish, lining them up next to mine. Her feet are bare and pink, her toes curling on the rug. There's a childlike vulnerability about her.

"Would you like water?" I ask, heading to the kitchenette.

"No, thanks." She follows me, surveying every inch of the space. "You live here with your fiancé?"

I nod. "Part-time and in the main house. He's in forestry—working the Rim this summer." I hear myself babbling, so I change course. "I know Willow already told you, but Ashiatsu is not as weird as it sounds. There are bars in the ceiling that I hold onto so I'm never actually walking on you. And you can stop me at any time if it's too much."

"I trust you," she says, and I almost laugh at the irony.

She lays her purse on the counter, watching me with the stillness of a heron. There's something about her: the way she's always reading the room, calculating, two steps ahead.

I try to reset from my morning's trauma and back into the role of massage therapist—the calm voice, the measured breath, the confident hands. I guide her slowly down the hall and into the therapy room.

"I leave you here to undress," I say, reciting the script. "Face-down under the sheet, I'll knock before I come in."

She gives me a curt nod. "Thanks."

I close the door behind her, then collapse against it, my pulse pounding in my ears before I move to the bathroom where I scrub my feet and slip them into clean soft slippers. I grab my brush and run it through my hair, pulling it up into a ponytail. With one quick splash of water on my face, I pat it dry and give a few spritzes of rose water. I take another look after quickly changing my coffee-stained shirt into a workout tank top. There, it's almost as though none of the murder business took place this morning.

Giving her a few more minutes, I concentrate on my breath and count several times as I take deep breaths in and out. I feel so much calmer as I rap gently at the door.

"Ready," Joanne's voice drifts through the door, small and tentative.

I step inside, flip on the soft piano music, and line up with the overhead bars in ritual precision.

Joanne settles onto the face cradle, arms tucked in, hair

fanning across. I begin with light compressions, working warming oil into her shoulders. My hands know this dance by muscle memory.

For the first ten minutes, I'm on autopilot: kneading out the thick, ropey knots in her back, adjusting pressure until she emits a tiny, approving grunt. I keep my voice steady. "Pressure okay?"

She inhales. "It's perfect. You can go deeper."

Switching to the overhead bars, I slide my feet into position and start the Ashiatsu—heels rolling over her scapula in time with the faint rise and fall of her breath. Her body gradually melts under my weight.

About thirty minutes in, my mind unspools. I see the dead man's blue-tinged hands on that linoleum floor, the detective's clipped question: "Ever been here before, Ms. Madsen?" My heel slips for a heartbeat, and I almost lose my balance.

Joanne lifts her head slightly off the table, but says nothing.

"Sorry," I murmur, regaining my stance. "Slick spot."

I work in silence through the last strokes along her spine. I guide her to turn onto her back; she does so with surprising grace. From that moment, she turns talkative.

She thanks me for helping get her away from her sister, Willow, for the afternoon.

"One thing I understand well and that's overbearing sisters," I mention.

"I want to get to know her more, but sheesh. She just doesn't know when to quit."

"I got the impression you two spent a lot of years apart—you aren't close?"

"Well, when we were really little, we were inseparable.

She holds on to those days. I ran away from home ultimately—young and dumb. But also, our daddy wasn't the nicest person, so there was a reason for it."

"Oh. That must have been tough. Where'd you go?"

She pauses, and I assume she won't answer. Then, her chest rose as she inhaled deeply. "I met a guy. The love of my life. Until…"

Again, a huge long pause. I keep working on her legs, giving her the time.

"I—I don't usually," she murmurs in a low voice.

I give her a moment before resuming a gentle stretch, watching her breathing increase and realizing she had teared up. "It's about him," she whispers. "My husband."

"Oh?"

Her jaw clenches, then relaxes, sharing the weight of what she's been carrying. "He disappeared some time ago," she says, voice cracking. "We'd had a terrible fight—more than I've admitted to myself. He always hated staying in one place. Then one day he was just gone." She presses a hand to her collarbone as though pushing away a chill. "I miss him so much, even on the days when I remember how mean he could be."

My feet slowly moved over her quadriceps in slow, soothing sweeps. "That must have been terrifying,"

"Terrifying," she repeats, the single word hanging between us. "I wake up half hoping he'll walk through the door. But another part of me knows it's better this way. Willow says it is. She never liked him. Says he kept me away from the family all these years."

"Is that true?"

"Maybe. There's so much about our relationship, and I don't want to bore you with the details. I wish Willow would leave it alone, though. It's none of her business, and although she's an angel for letting me stay with her now, I don't know how I could stay much longer if she doesn't back off."

"I understand. I bet she's not so unlike my own sister. Well, I'm happy you came for some Ashiatsu therapy today then. Sounds like you really need it." I gently step down from the table, finish with a light palm press across her sternum, then step back.

Her eyes are closed when I step out of the room. I resist glancing into the hallway mirror—my reflection looks as raw as the stories I've heard today. Maybe I am a little haunted, too.

When Joanne finally emerges from the room, her cheeks are flushed, hair tousled. I hand her a glass of water, and she stands straighter, the tension gone from her jaw.

"Thank you," she says in a soft drawl. "That felt so nice." She hesitates, then adds, "I'm sorry. I've been thinking about him a lot lately, so I haven't exactly been myself. It's been a big adjustment for me, you know."

I reach out to hug the frail woman. When I pull back, I look her in the eyes. "I'm so sorry. But can I ask ... have the authorities been involved to find him?"

She shakes her head. "No. He left me. As simple as that." Then she crouches to pat Shadow's head—my old friend padding in on cue. The dog leans into her, tail thudding.

I sink to one knee, rubbing Shadow's ears. "I'm here," I tell Joanne. "Anytime you'd like to talk. Would you like to schedule another session?"

We check our calendars, and I book her for a two-hour session a few days out.

Joanne gives me a small, grateful smile, then slips out the door with a soft click. I watch her drive away, vanishing amongst the pines until the hush returns.

Shadow pads back and drops her chin into my lap. I stroke her warm fur, feeling the day's weight settle into my bones: the body in Show Low, the detective's overly pushy questions, Joanne's tabletop confession. What a day.

But right now, here's a cuddly dog, a clean house, and I survived today.

CHAPTER TWELVE

It's barely five a.m. and Shadow has already made three laps around the backyard, sniffed the fire pit, and attempted to dig up whatever rodent graveyard lies beneath the patio stones. I watch her through the glass of the French doors, clutching my mug of reheated coffee, willing my brain to stop replaying yesterday's trauma.

Today is supposed to be different. My sister and her daughters—my twin nieces, freshly thirteen and flush with the hormonal angst of the newly minted teenager— are due to arrive for a week-long mountain adventure. I haven't told Jordan about the murder, or the theft, or the impromptu brush with law enforcement. Why would I when nothing makes you look like a lunatic quite as fast as, "Oh, by the way, your sister, and guardian of your children for the next week, just stumbled into a crime scene."

Greg's gone for an early morning run, taking advantage of the clear air before the sun gets high enough to bake the forest. I hear his footfalls on the deck about the same time Shadow barks at something only she can see in the neighbor's yard. I tug on the door and step outside, greeting him with the best smile I can muster.

He squints into the sun, brow glistening with sweat. "You survived the night," he says, only half joking.

"Barely. Did you know that there is no such thing as 'sleeping in' when you live in the woods? Every bird in Arizona is in on some kind of dawn chorus conspiracy."

He grins and plucks a weed from the garden bed, tossing it over the railing. "I'll set up the grill for later. You want me to pick up anything from the store before your sister gets here?"

"No, we're covered."

We head back inside, Shadow hot on our heels, and I spend the next hours blitz-cleaning the living room and searching for errant socks and hairbands that have somehow already migrated under the couch. Tidying the guest bedrooms with fresh sheets, vacuuming, and scouring bathrooms is an excellent distraction from checking the phone every ten seconds.

At exactly eleven a.m., a blue Outback with a dented fender comes crunching up the driveway. My sister Jordan is at the wheel, cell phone wedged between her shoulder and ear, mouthing 'one sec' to me as she swings the car door open. The twins burst from the backseat with the velocity of live ammunition.

Apple—tall, with a splash of freckles across her nose—bounds out of the car with her duffel and canvas tote, her face lighting up when she spots me. "Aunt Libby!" she calls out, dropping her bags to rush forward for a hug before reluctantly pulling back to check a notification on her phone. She swipes her long, straight blonde hair behind her right ear.

Annie, meanwhile, does a cartwheel on the gravel and sticks the landing all while her blonde ponytail bounces wildly. Shadow barks, spinning in delighted circles.

"Hey, guys! No blood yet? Good start."

Jordan, now off the phone, sweeps in for a quick hug and a squinting inspection of my face. "You look like hell," she whispers. "Did you go out last night?"

"Kind of," I say, squeezing her tight. "More like 'survived a harrowing ordeal and then downed three glasses of wine.' You?"

"Three hours in the car with these monsters, so yes." She gestures with her keys to the girls.

I usher everyone inside, feigning domestic competence. "I made muffins for a snack. They're gluten-free and probably taste like recycled cardboard, but it's the thought that counts."

Apple gives me a sideways glance. "Is there actual cardboard in these, or are you just being dramatic?"

I wink. "Why not both?"

They pile into the kitchen, and Greg appears just in time to snag a muffin for himself.

"Ladies," he says, bowing with an exaggerated flourish. "Please make yourselves at home. Shadow's just shed her spring coat all over the couch, so if anyone needs extra insulation—"

"I'll take it!" Annie grabs Shadow in a bear hug, grinning. "She smells like campfire. I love it."

I offer drinks and snacks to the group, slipping into my role as hostess while burying the memory of yesterday's police station visit. If Jordan picks up on my unease, she doesn't say a word. Instead, she beams with pride as she recounts Apple's stellar report card.

"You wouldn't believe it, Lib! Straight A's this year! She's basically a genius," she exclaims, her eyes sparkling with maternal pride. "And you should have seen her when she got the news—she practically floated out of the school!"

As Jordan continues to rave about Apple's academic achievements, I can't help but smile, momentarily distracted from the chaos swirling in my mind.

Annie interrupts, her eyes bright with excitement. "Can I take Shadow outside? I want to play fetch!"

Greg chuckles, leaning against the counter. "Just make sure you keep an eye on her, okay?"

With that, Annie darts out the door, calling for Shadow, who bounds after her with joyful yips. Apple watches them go, shaking her head with a smirk.

I slide the plate of muffins toward her, the warm aroma wafting through the kitchen. "How about a snack before they create chaos outside?"

Apple picks one up, taking a cautious bite. "These aren't half bad, Aunt Libby."

Jordan smiles, though her eyes flicker, thinking of the day ahead. "I wish I could stay longer, but I need to head back to Mesa soon." She picks at a muffin, mood suddenly heavier. "You ever wish we were still kids? Like, just for a day?"

I look at the table—crumbs, mismatched cups, two generations of Madsen women under one roof, if only briefly. "No. But sometimes I wish we knew less about the world."

She gives a soft, half-hearted laugh. "Well, we're giving the girls that illusion for a week. You're the cool aunt now, Libby. Don't screw it up."

I breathe in, exhale, and for the first time all day, the anxiety eases. Family is chaos, but at least it's a familiar one.

* * *

Within several hours, the outside deck fills with the savory scent of burgers sizzling on the grill, mingling with the faint aroma of wood smoke. Apple and Annie bustle around the kitchen with me, their laughter echoing as we chop lettuce, slice ripe tomatoes, and fill bowls with crunchy chips. It feels like a return to simpler times, the kind of busywork that quiets the mind and draws us together.

Greg is outside at the grill, flipping patties with the same meticulous care he usually reserves for his Forest Service reports. Apple claims a spot by the kitchen window, while Annie hums a cheerful tune, darting between the counter and the fridge, gathering condiments and keeping Shadow entertained with playful antics.

We load up paper plates and carry our feast outside. We settle at the picnic table, surrounded by the gentle hum of the whispering pines swaying in the breeze.

"Here's to mountain summers," I raise my glass.

Annie giggles, her mouth full of burger. "We can actually be outside!"

I laugh, feeling lighter. Shadow flops at our feet, her tail thumping against the ground.

Just then, Willow strolls through the backyard from the side of the house, her presence brightening the scene. "Hey, everyone! Smells amazing!" She leans against the porch railing, casually joining in. "I just saw Beth at the center. The police were interviewing her … I'm assuming it's about the storage theft?"

The mention of the police sends a ripple of tension through me, but I try brushing it off. "Oh, just small-town drama, right?" I give my head a tilt toward the girls on my left. "By the way, I've got to introduce you to my nieces—this is Apple, and next to her is Annie."

Willow greets them with her warm smile. "So nice to meet you, young ladies. Having fun with Aunt Libby?" she asks, making her way up the steps to join us at the table.

"It's so nice here!" Annie exclaims. "And we get to help at some fair this weekend."

"Oh, that's fantastic! We need all the help we can get."

I offer Willow a cheeseburger, but she declines, saying she had a late lunch. She chatters on while we busily enjoy our late lunch-early dinner. By the time I finish the last potato chip on my plate, I give her a look to join me as I clear the others' dishes.

As soon as we're out of earshot, I question my friend. "What did Beth tell you? I've tried to get hold of her, but she's not answering her phone."

Her eyes shoot past me, looking through the windows, then answers softly. "Nothing really. What happened in Show Low, Libby?"

"The address that Beth sent me to led me right into the middle of a murder scene. That's what happened."

She gasps, her hand slapping across her mouth all in one movement. "Murder?" she whispers. "Why did she send you to Show Low?"

I explain about the donation for the silent auction and walk her through my entire day, stopping short of revealing the massage her sister came over for.

"And they think you had something to do with it?"

"I'm not sure. But let me tell you—I sure got the interrogation!" I grab a nearby towel to wipe off the countertop. "I had nothing to do with it; I have no idea who the man was. There's no evidence other than I was in the wrong place at the wrong time."

Saying it aloud made me realize how frequently I'm in the wrong place at the wrong time. I scrub the countertop even harder. "I mean, c'mon, I've never heard of any of them—the ones police questioned me about—Spiegel, Blankenship, or Sanchez. There's no way they can tie me to any of them, so I have nothing to worry about, do I?"

I look up from my frenzied counter wiping to see Willow's face white as a sheet. "What? What is it?" I put the towel down and came around the counter, touching her arm.

She pulls away, grabs at her sweater and wraps it tighter around her. "Nothing. Uh, I just remembered, I've gotta get back." Her eyes search the nearby table, and then again through the glass doors outside. "My purse must be in the car." She hurries toward the back door. "Look, Libby, I hope everything turns out okay for you. I've gotta go." And with that, she hastily retreats through the backyard, saying quick goodbyes to Greg and the girls.

Following her through the door, I watch the last sight of her long brown hair as she disappears around the corner of the house.

Greg looks up at me. "Wow, she was in a hurry. I thought she might join us for some dessert."

"I know. That was weird."

"What happened?"

Not wanting to bring up the subject of yesterday in

front of the girls, I make light of it and simply explain that Willow's a busy lady.

Soon after, Greg brings out a tub of rocky road ice cream and assists the girls in assembling s'mores over the hot grill, their excitement bubbling over. I watch from the kitchen as they create a delightful mess, laughter filling the air.

Punching the button on my phone, I try one more time to reach Beth. Still no luck, so I join the summer ice cream and s'mores party outside and try to put behind the unease in my gut.

For a few minutes, the anxiety slips away, replaced by the light-hearted competition of who can eat more ice cream before brain freeze sets in. Greg drapes an arm around my shoulders, and I lean into him, letting the worries of the week fade away.

"Libby, you're doing great," he murmurs in his soothing voice.

I squeeze his hand, grateful for his support. "Thanks, I really appreciate it."

As the evening unfolds, I look over to see the twins sprawling out on the grass, their bare feet brushing against each other as they debate whether they'll be able to see the constellations overhead. It reminds me of summers with my sister at their same age. Apple insists light pollution will make it impossible to enjoy, declaring it's merely a "cloud of atmospheric particulates."

Their playful back-and-forth brings a smile to my face, filling me with warmth and reminding me of the joy found in these small, youthful moments. This is what I want to cherish from this summer—the laughter, the delightful chaos of having kids around, the feeling of being fully alive with my family.

Greg joins me, the warmth of the late afternoon settling around us. He nudges me playfully. "Tomorrow will be easier."

My eyes find his, and for the first time in ages, I almost believe it might be true.

CHAPTER THIRTEEN

The following day starts with a chorus of voices I'm unaccustomed to, but which immediately brings excitement to my heart.

Shadow follows the girls into the kitchen with the enthusiasm of a retriever on a breakfast mission. I greet them, already three sips into my first cup of coffee and deep in the trenches of a French toast production.

Greg, who claims to need quiet in the morning but secretly loves the energy, slips onto the patio with his own mug and a couple of dog biscuits for Shadow. I sprinkle cinnamon sugar over the pan and try to ignore the low rumble of dread remaining in my gut from yesterday's drama.

The table fills up fast: Annie first, fork in hand and

already negotiating extra syrup rations; Apple next, hair in a nice tidy ponytail and eyes fixed on her phone; Greg last, but only after refilling his mug.

"So," I say to the girls, while flipping another slice of French toast, "are you two ready for work today? I'm not sure what your assignments will be, but you might be involved in the setting up for the ball at some point."

Annie's eyes go wide. "The ball? Is the decorating already started?"

I nod. "They're doing a test run of the lighting and sound system. The tables will all have to be set up, and I'm sure there's decorating to do."

Apple shrugs, which is her way of saying she's already made her peace with the schedule.

Greg sets his mug down. "You girls brought dresses, right?"

Annie rolls her eyes. "Duh. It's a ball."

Greg chuckles and then takes another sip of coffee.

Apple, cheeks blushing, stares pointedly at the French toast, but there's the twinge of a smile at the corners of her mouth. "So, are you and Greg going? You'll be chaperoning, right?"

"Of course," I say, hoping my voice doesn't betray the fact that, lately, I can barely keep my own life together, let alone keep an eye on two adolescent teens.

The voice of my sister's last words before she left still haunts me: "Don't you dare let my daughters out of your sight, or so help me." And how she waited until Annie was distracted by her phone before adding, "They're a little boy crazy these days. Not that they'd admit it. But just … you know. Be vigilant."

Greg grins at the girls, ruffles Annie's hair, and says, "Who's ready for the festival today? Rumor has it the local fire chief is bringing in an entire crew."

Annie, ever the extrovert, is practically vibrating. "Are we allowed to talk to them?"

Greg shrugs. "You can, but you'll probably be too busy signing people up for the pie-eating contest."

Apple perks up. "Is there really a pie-eating contest?"

"Every year," I say. "And they crown a champion with an actual whipped cream crown. It's a big deal."

Apple smiles, glancing at Annie. "I dare you."

"I double dare you."

We eat in a noisy rush; the girls wolfing down the French toast like they're fueling for a marathon. Then, I clear the plates, wipe the table, and as the girls retreat to their bedroom, I'm reminded what good kids they are. This won't be an issue.

The twins reappear half an hour later, Apple in a hoodie and black leggings, Annie in a sequin-studded t-shirt that reads Sparkle Authority. They're ready for anything. I grab my keys, leash up Shadow, and shepherd everyone out the door.

As I turn onto the main road, I realize my mind's elsewhere. The fundraiser, the crowds, the thought of being responsible for two actual human children for an entire week. It's enough to make anyone nervous. But I'm looking forward to it. What I'm more nervous about is whether the fundraiser will earn enough money despite the thefts.

Annie is a never-ending stream of questions. "Will we *really* get to meet the firefighters? What if I win the pie contest? What is a silent auction anyway?" She pauses only to take a selfie, which she immediately Snapchats to everyone.

Apple, from the back: "Is there Wi-Fi at the community center?"

I laugh. "I'm sure you'll be plenty busy enough. There won't be time for playing on your phones."

We pull into the gravel lot and it's already packed—SUVs, minivans, and the occasional tricked-out Jeep with enough bumper stickers to start a philosophy debate. Volunteers are milling around in matching t-shirts and sun hats; Willow is waving a clipboard like a traffic director; Beth stands at the entrance with a bullhorn and a fanny pack.

Annie claps her hands, eager with anticipation. "Let's do this!"

I check my phone one last time, then take a breath and lead them into the fray.

Beth spots us and swoops in for a hug, clipboard smacking my shoulder. "Libby! You made it!"

Shadow barks with excitement.

I stifle a laugh. "Of course. I've tried calling…"

She immediately interjects, surveying the girls. "These must be your assistants you've been telling me about?"

Annie and Apple look at each other, then at Beth, then both say "yes" in perfect unison.

Beth grins. "Excellent. We've got jobs for everyone. Let's get you your volunteer t-shirts."

I try again to get her attention for a private conversation, but she quickly steers us to a table loaded with t-shirts in a variety of sizes and colors. Annie picks the brightest one in tie-dye; Apple selects black. I go for navy. Beth gives us all name tags ("Libby," "Annie," "Apple"—no pretense here) and runs down the assignments.

"Libby, you, Shadow, and Apple will man the 50/50

raffle desk just inside the entrance. Annie, you're with Willow for event setup and crowd wrangling. I think the pie-toss is your first gig."

Annie pumps a fist in the air. "Yes!"

I try to get her attention. "Beth…"

She brushes me off again. "Later, Libby. Right now, we need to focus on this," she says pointedly.

I glance at the girls, already lost in their new roles, and for the first time today, I feel a jolt of actual excitement. We're really doing this.

Beth hands me a walkie-talkie and winks. "You're officially in the club."

I decide to get into the spirit, leaving the other issues behind for today. I smile at her. "Bring it on."

Annie runs toward Willow, who's waving her over with dramatic arm gestures. I watch for a beat, then turn to Apple. "Ready?"

She grins. "Yes! Let's go sell some tickets!"

And just like that, the day begins.

By ten a.m. the main hall is packed, voices ricocheting off the cinderblock walls. I'm stationed at the folding table just inside the entrance, Apple at my right, a box of 50/50 tickets at the ready, and Shadow at my feet.

Apple has certainly mastered the art of upselling, selling the special 'five for ten' to nearly everyone who approaches. The range of customers proves eclectic, and we soon find ourselves in a people-watching game, one Shadow seems to enjoy the most.

Our first customer is a woman with hair the exact color of a traffic cone, wearing matching Crocs and a T-shirt that reads "Ask Me About My Llamas." She buys the special package, then attempts to upsell us on the merits of llama ownership for "brush control and spiritual grounding." Apple deadpans, "Can they be house trained?" and the woman launches into a ten-minute TED Talk about livestock diapers.

I keep a running tally of every ticket sold, impressed by Apple's ability to handle cash, make change, and gently create nicknames for the most interesting folks without them ever catching on. We meet a man in full Civil War re-enactor gear, who insists on paying with half-dollars ("It's tradition, miss")—his name for the weekend became Paul Revere.

A young woman who claims to have psychic powers and tries to predict our raffle numbers ("You have the aura of a three, but with the luck of an eight") earned the nickname of Claire.

The pair of teenage boys, both named Jaden, who dared each other to buy more tickets and then ran off giggling, she lovingly deemed them to be Giggles.

Apple collects all of this like blackmail material, scribbling notes on a sheet of scratch paper between sales. "I'm making a character list for my novel," she whispers. "Everyone is so much more interesting here."

"I'm pretty sure that woman is running a cult," I say, and receive a growl from Shadow.

Apple doesn't look up. "She's Claire-*voyant.*"

I marvel at her creativity, while Shadow gives a small whine.

Midday, Beth whooshes by. "How's my bestseller?" she asks, ruffling Apple's hair and then scanning my sales log. "You're ahead of last year's pace. If you keep this up, I'm naming you Volunteer Queen."

Apple grins. "Can I get a crown?"

"Only if you beat the fire chief," Beth says, and barrels off to the next crisis.

We take turns sneaking snacks from the volunteer lounge (bagels, mini muffins, and protein bites that taste mostly like peanut butter). Every hour, Shadow and I venture outside and check the pie booth, where Annie and Willow are living their best lives.

The pie station is in a makeshift pen outside, surrounded by hay bales and lines of children. The goal: pay a dollar to throw a whipped cream pie at a rotating selection of local celebrities, which today includes the elementary school principal, two town council members, and an off-duty police officer.

Annie, resplendent in her bright tie-dye volunteer t-shirt, is Willow's cheerleader. She shrieks, cackles, and generally incites the crowd, leading chants of "More! More! More!" with a voice that can cut through jet engine noise. Shadow jumps up and down, really wanting to join Annie.

Willow, wearing a trash bag as a cape, orchestrates the event like a mad scientist, handing out pies and coaching her customers in proper tossing technique.

Every time a pie lands, Annie howls in delight. By noon, both she and Willow are spattered with enough cream to suggest a dairy explosion. I watch Annie take a turn, nailing the principal square in the chin, then high-five a six-year-old so hard they almost fall over.

I check in, but Willow waves me off. "We've got this, Libby! She's a natural." Annie looks so proud, face sticky and eyes bright.

When Apple sneaks out on break and surveys the carnage, she comes back saying, "They're like evil twins," she says, about Annie and Willow.

"She's in her element," I reply.

Apple shrugs. "I kind of envy her."

At the ticket table, where the afternoon rush is in full swing, I catch up with a few locals. They recount the town's ancient scandals (last year's stolen gnome epidemic; the infamous snowplow theft of '08), and try to recruit me for their respective causes. I think I have enough of my own scandals to deal with at the moment, but thankfully they seem none the wiser. Most of them seem much more interested in petting Shadow, and she sure loves it.

A guy with a handlebar mustache and a stained Hot Dog Hut polo wants to know if I'm from around here. As Shadow sniffs him up and down, sure he must still have a hot dog on him somewhere, I explain how I'm just visiting for the summer, and he gives a knowing nod. "Careful, this place grows on you," he says, wagging a ticket stub. "Next thing you know, you'll be on a committee."

After the pie-throwing contest, and while on break, Annie signs up for the infamous pie-eating contest at the last possible minute. Before I have any say in the matter, she slams her way through three full pies before hitting the wall. She finishes a fourth one, but only receives a special spirit award for enthusiasm, which she wears around her neck with pride. Willow gives her a standing ovation.

Afterward, we regroup in the volunteer lounge. Annie has a crust of cream on her, but she is beaming. Apple is quieter, but her eyes are bright as she picks at a lemon bar and scrolls through photos on her phone.

"You killed it out there," I say, nudging Annie.

She grins, her cheeks pink. "I wanna do it again tomorrow."

"Let's see how you feel about that in the morning." I

figure she'll be sick and will never want to see pie again.

Beth swings by to check on us, eyes darting everywhere. "You good?" she asks.

"We're great," I say. "But can I speak to you in private?"

"Yeah, we need to chat. Give me a few minutes and I'll meet you in the office." Then she turns to the group of us, leaning in and says, "I meant it earlier—thank you for all this. You've saved my butt more than once today."

I shake my head. "We're happy to help."

Apple pipes up, "We're coming back tomorrow, right?"

I glance at both girls, tired but alive in a way I haven't seen in months. "Definitely."

After Beth heads off, I see Willow approaching. I pull her aside, asking if she can watch the girls for a little longer. She readily agrees and piques their interest when she mentions a firefighter calendar photo-op going on across the way. I watch the three of them as they hurriedly walk away.

Shadow and I wait in the office for Beth. After twenty minutes, I'm ready to give up and stand to leave. Beth could have been an Arizona dust devil the way she blows into the room apologizing for lateness. She receives a warning bark for causing my dog a fright.

"Beth, what on earth is going on?"

"Well, Libby … I've been a little overwhelmed with the event. If you haven't noticed, it's a little crazy."

"No, no. Not that. I'm freaking out about finding a dead body at the place you sent me to!"

"Oh, *that*."

"I've left you messages, and I need to know what you told the police. Do I need to hire a lawyer? Who was that guy—where you sent me?"

Beth sighs. "I don't know, Libby. I'm as baffled as you are." She points to a chair, indicating I should retake my seat. She pulls out hers and sits. Shadow is still on alert, clearly not sure about the energy in the room.

"Do you know the man who died?" I ask.

"No."

"Did we have the wrong address?"

"Apparently. I asked the cops whether they had found a box of coins at the crime scene, for our charity organization. They found no coins at all. So, either it was a hoax—or someone gave us the wrong address. I don't know."

"Or someone stole the coins and killed a man over them?"

"Ohhh. I hadn't gone to that extreme conclusion. Are you okay, Libby?"

"Beth, I don't know what to think. But it sounds like our stories match up. I was running an errand for you— neither of us knows anything about the deceased or the homeowner."

She nods.

I lean in. "Should I be worried? So much has happened since I've started volunteering. First, someone takes the storage locker keys and uses them to steal a valuable statue. Next, someone breaks into the community center … and I'm still wondering how those two things might be connected. Then, a simple errand to pick up a donation results in finding a dead body!"

"I know. I know. It's been unfortunate, but the police are working on each case, and we'll wait to see what they learn. In the meantime, we have this fundraiser to get through. And hopefully we earn enough for the firefighters." Her expression darkens.

"What? What is it?"

"I just remembered." She clears her throat before continuing. "There's chatter about the artist who donated the expensive sculpture. There could be a lawsuit."

"Suing us?"

"Well, they are going after the town for not securing…" she hems and haws a moment. "Ugh, there are rumblings about personal…"

I cut her off. "Are they coming after *me*?"

"Now, Libby … I don't think they…"

"Beth! I didn't *do* anything!"

"*Well*, you had the keys…"

"Ok, but that doesn't mean someone didn't steal the key from the ring. I sure didn't take it off. Remember that day we discovered the theft, when I tried the keys in the lock, *none* of them worked. Who stole the key from the ring?"

Silence. It was clearly the first time she'd seen it in this light. Before she can respond, someone knocks on the door and steps into the room.

"Beth, there's a runaway llama from the petting zoo…"

"Oh geez. I'll be right there. Libby, we're going to have to table this for now. I appreciate your insight, and I will follow up. Don't worry, everything will work out."

She hurries out the door, leaving me sitting there shaking my head. I've heard similar platitudes too many times recently. In my experience, I know not to depend on others. It's up to me to save my own rear end.

That's when something else dawns on me.

Shadow and I work our way through the crowd inside and find the girls still admiring the firefighters.

Willow steps back from them, and nudges me. "There

are so many good-looking ones, aren't there?"

I nod. I mean, I don't care who you are. How could I deny that as they posed in varying photos with members of the community?

"Hey, Willow. How do you know Marty Spiegel?"

Her head whipped around. "What?"

"When I mentioned yesterday that, during the police interrogation, I didn't know the people they questioned me about?"

"Uh, yeah."

"When I mentioned the last names, you clearly recognized at least one."

"Uh, I'm not sure what you mean."

"C'mon, Willow. Something I said struck a chord with you. What was it?"

She glances right, then left. "I don't know what to tell you. It was probably my shock at what you told me. It's not everyday someone tells you about witnessing something like that."

That could be true, but for whatever reason, I don't believe her. I only nod and let her and the girls know that we've gotta get going. Begrudgingly, the twins pull themselves away and we head out to the parking lot.

On the way home, Annie regales us with a blow-by-blow of every pie hit ("the principal totally let me win"), while Apple quietly hums along to a playlist she won't admit to liking.

I park in the driveway with a quick glance at the back seats. The twins lean their heads together. Shadow's tail thumps against the seat in time with their laughter.

Overall, today was a win.

CHAPTER FOURTEEN

If yesterday was a win, today must be some kind of universal test. The town's population seems to have doubled overnight, with visitors flooding in from every corner of Rim Country. By nine a.m., every parking space within a half mile of the community center is full. Volunteers in neon vests direct traffic with the resigned despair of people who've already given up on their own safety.

Inside, the building thrums with the electric haze of anticipation. Vendors hawk everything from Navajo fry bread to $6 lemonade; outside on the expansive grounds, the school jazz band sets up on the main stage, tuning instruments at maximum volume.

Shadow is excited by all the commotion, but stays right

at my side on her leash. Once we hunt down Beth, trying her best to remain calm, we get our assignments for the day.

Apple is working the technology table today, with an actual laptop and a badge that says Tech Goddess. She takes her role seriously, directing patrons to the correct password when trying to access the community center Wi-Fi ("Try all lowercase. It's fireball2025."), and answering questions when vendor QR codes won't work. I check in every hour, but she's clearly in her element, helping those who need it and otherwise ignoring the world around her.

Annie, on the other hand, is in the children's activity zone, paired again with Willow and a rotating cast of helpers. Today's assignment: face painting and what Beth described as 'creative supervision.' Willow sets up a table with a hundred little paint pots, and Annie is instantly the Picasso for the under-10 set. I never knew her to be a great little artist, but seeing the creativity—elaborate cartoon-like animals, superhero masks, and—on one very lucky toddler—a glittery unicorn—I was quite impressed.

I spend the first half of the day shuttling between my assignment at the silent auction, where I police sticky-fingered teens and entertain older adult bidders with small talk—er, instructions for the auction rules. The event is in full swing, and those interested in the auction find themselves distracted by Shadow. Which works perfectly because every twenty minutes, a fresh crisis requires managing: a tipped-over beverage, a missing pen, a dramatic confrontation over whether the "vintage Barbie" is truly vintage.

By three o'clock, the sun is high and the hall is at its maximum capacity. Beth finds Shadow and me in the volunteer lounge, stress-eating a bag of baby carrots and dog cookies.

"Libby, quick question," she says, voice tight. "Have you seen Willow?"

I shake my head. "Last I checked, she and Annie were with the face painting group."

Beth's fear washes over her face. "She's not there. Neither is Annie."

A wave of icy panic slaps me in the chest. "How long?"

Beth glances at her phone. "Twenty minutes, maybe more?"

"Maybe they took a break? Or they're on the lawn?" Shadow and I are already moving, out the door and down the main hall, scanning every cluster of participants for blonde ponytails or the flash of her tie-dye shirt. The activity room is packed, but I don't find Willow or Annie anywhere. I feel a bead of sweat building on my brow.

Apple is at her table, tapping on her phone. "Where's your sister?" I ask, trying to keep the panic out of my voice.

She shrugs, but I see her eyes flicker with worry. "Haven't seen her."

"Did she have her phone?"

Apple holds up her own, already typing. "I'll try texting her."

I make a loop outside, calling Annie's name, my voice thin and desperate. We continue looping through the grounds, checking the food court, the vendor tents, and the parking lot. No Annie, no Willow. I try Willow's cell, but it goes straight to voicemail. Each time I circle back to the building, the noise seems louder, the heat more oppressive.

I return to the lounge, hoping for news. Nothing.

At some point, I see a familiar face in the crowd—a woman in dark sunglasses, wearing a pale blue parka despite the heat, with her stringy gray hair pulled tight. She's staring at me, the line of her jaw sharp and still. It takes me a moment, but then I remember: it's the neighbor from the Show Low mobile home park. The one who called me a liar. She's halfway across the room, but when she sees me, she ducks behind the soft pretzel stand.

My heart rate spikes. *Was she following me?* I force myself to stay on task—find Annie first—but the sight of that woman sticks in my brain like a splinter.

A volunteer in a cactus hat shuffles up to me, holding a walkie-talkie. "Beth says to check the south lawn, near the dunk tank," she says. "She heard they might have gone there."

I thank her and head outside, weaving through kids with balloons and parents arguing over sunscreen. The south lawn is crowded; a throng of people, mostly tweens and teens, are pressed up against the makeshift stage. There, in the center of the mob, is the answer to my panic.

A group of firefighters, half in uniform and half—alarmingly—shirtless, are performing in a Firefighter Challenge talent show. They're running obstacle courses, doing push-ups, and, currently, flexing in a choreographed dance to *Uptown Funk*. The crowd is losing its mind.

And there, front row center, are Annie and Willow, both cheering like they're at a rock concert. Annie is up on Willow's shoulders, waving something in the air like a victory flag.

I shove through the crowd; a tidal wave of relief combined with irritation floods my system. I grab Willow by the arm, and Annie looks down from her perch and squeals, "Aunt Libby! They're doing a dance-off! It's hilarious."

"I've been looking all over for you!" I hiss, but my voice is more relief than anger.

Willow, looking abashed, but not really regretful. "Sorry, Libby. She said she had to see it. You're right, we should have told you."

I fix Annie with a glare. "Your mother will kill me if you go missing." As the words leave my mouth, I know I have to tone it down.

Willow gives a sheepish grin. "Next time we'll text."

I can feel the last of my panic draining away. More relaxed, and relieved I've found them, I join them with a few catcalls for the performing men up on the stage. Annie hugs me, not letting go even when the crowd chants for an encore. Willow gives me a side-hug, too, and for a moment we're just three idiots, enjoying the sight of the hunky firefighters.

I check my phone and see three missed calls from Jordan, which I ignore for now. When we finally walk back inside, Apple is waiting at the technology table, watching us approach with her arms folded and a look that says, "I told you so."

We regroup in the lounge with Annie breathlessly recounting every moment of the talent show, while Apple rolls her eyes but is clearly happy her sister wasn't actually lost. I collapse in a plastic chair, watching the girls eat popsicles.

Beth pops in with a clipboard, sweat streaming down her face. "You found them!"

I nod, too tired to elaborate.

She grins. "You're a hero, Libby."

I shake my head since the situation really doesn't warrant it, but, weirdly, I almost feel like one.

CHAPTER FIFTEEN

Before I can even gather the girls, or sneak a single bite of carrot cake in the volunteer lounge, I spot her again through the opened door—pale blue parka, purse strap wound twice around her wrist, lurking just inside the main entrance of the community center. Her eyes dart over the crowd like she's scanning it for someone.

The neighbor from Mitchell Road. The one who'd called me a liar. She's shorter than I recall, hunched over and looking timid in a room jammed with bodies. Shadow registers her presence first, hackles up, ears pricked, tail tucked between her legs.

I excuse myself from the others, maneuvering my way across the foyer, sidestepping toddlers, and dodging the line for the cotton candy cart, before stopping short of her personal space. She smells faintly of cigarette smoke. Up close, I see her hands tremble, nails bitten raw. She tries not to look at me, but fails.

"Hi," I say, softly as I can. "You're—uh, I think we met last week?"

She freezes, then gives a jerky nod, eyes wide behind oversized sunglasses. "Yes. You're the lady from the …" She wobbles her hand, as if conjuring up the right word.

"From the trailer park," I add. "Mitchell Road." Keeping my voice down, not wanting to create a scene, I introduce myself. "I'm Libby Madsen. I don't think we've met."

She hesitates, then lifts her chin. "I'm Patty," she says. "I'm really sorry, I shouldn't even—" She glances over her shoulder, as if expecting someone to haul her away. "It's been kind of a week."

"I get it," I say, and Shadow leans in to sniff her sneakers, tail swishing in a tentative half-circle. "It's been a week here, too." I try to smile, but it comes out crooked. "Sorry for, you know, all the drama the other day."

She shrugs, as if it's the price of living in a place where you can see five neighbors from your window and hear every domestic dispute through the tin walls.

"I'm not sure I'm supposed to talk to you," she whispers. "I just … I told the police, but I'm afraid people think you're involved."

"I'm not. I was there to pick up a donation—for this event, actually. Nothing more."

Patty gives me a long, searching look, then lets out a nervous laugh. "And instead, you found a dead body."

"Yeah," I say. "Not my best errand run."

She chews her lower lip, her gaze flicking from me to

Shadow and then back to the ground. "I saw the cops at Marty's place again this morning. They were taking pictures of the mailbox." She shudders. "Did you know that guy who stayed with him?"

I slowly shake my head. "Do you? Do you know his name?"

"No," she says. "Not really. I mean, I saw that guy around a few times. He was always working on cars for cash. Stayed over at Marty's sometimes." She picks at a thread on her sleeve. "I just never thought he'd … uh, end up like that. Seemed like a decent guy."

I take a step closer. "Have you seen Marty since?"

Patty goes stiff. "No. I don't remember exactly when it was—a week or more, that's what I told police, anyway. He waved to me, but he was loading his truck and on his way out. He does claims adjusting, you know. Drives all over the Rim for work."

I blink. "He's an insurance adjuster?" A chill ran up my spine, thinking of the last debacle I got myself into. My late father was an insurance adjuster.

She nods. "Fire, flood, mostly. Sometimes he'll be gone two, three days straight. That's why the police asked me—about who had the key. But Marty doesn't even lock the door half the time, I told them." Her voice drops to a whisper. "You think he's a suspect?"

I shrug. "I don't know."

"Do you know someone with the last name Sanchez in your neighborhood?"

She considers the question for a second, and then hesitantly moves her head. "Nope."

Shadow sits on her haunches and rests her head on Patty's calf, the world's gentlest canine pressure point. The neighbor reaches down and pets her without thinking.

"I'm scared," she says, barely louder than the hum of the soda machines. "I know it's dumb, but what if whoever did it comes back?" She hunches as if expecting a bullet from the popcorn stand.

"I really doubt that will happen," I say, wishing my voice could sound more convincing.

She gives me a look: *Yeah, right.*

I try again for more information. "Did Marty and his friend get along?"

She nods. "Seemed to …" She struggles for words, then adds, "Seems like they were business partners of some sort, but not in the insurance business. Marty said the guy was the only one who understood engines better than he did." Her expression turned.

"What is it?"

"Well, I did witness a few things. Saw them arguing a couple times. I told the detective all this already."

I file that away. "And no one else came by Marty's place?"

She shakes her head. "Not that I know of. Except maybe the guy who was over there last month, I think. Tall, wore glasses, and he had a vest on, like he was ready to go fishing or something."

"Were you ever introduced to him?"

"No. But he drove an old sedan with Nevada plates."

Interesting. "You saw him the morning of …?"

She frowns. "No, several weeks before. That day I didn't see anyone except you."

I watch the way her fingers tap at her elbow, rapid and irregular, like she's counting down to something awful. "Do you want to sit down?" I ask. "I can get you a water or—"

She recoils a little. "No, I just—" She glances toward the exit, then back at me, then at the row of vending machines. "I need to get back. I'm supposed to watch my granddaughter after this."

"Just one more question?"

She nods.

"Whose dog is Tiger?"

"Marty's."

"Not a neighbor who lives several places down? That's what another lady said that day."

"No, definitely Marty's dog. Poor guy."

"And where is the dog now?"

"With another neighbor until Marty gets home."

I nod, satisfied that the dog was being looked after. "And if you think of anything else, here—" I scribble my cell on the back of a napkin. "Text or call anytime."

She folds it neatly, then tucks it in her pocket. "Alright then."

As she walks off, Shadow gives a quiet whine, watching her leave as if she knows there's something sad in the way the woman hurries for the door.

I watch, too. And even as I turn to find the girls, my mind is buzzing. I wonder what the police were doing to find Marty Spiegel? And what about this new information—the guy from Nevada—could there be a link there? And, most of all, is there a connection between the stolen sculpture, a missing key, and the murder on Mitchell Road?

I don't have an answer. But I'd definitely like to put it all behind me so I could enjoy my summer in the mountains, and the week-long visit with my nieces.

I finally wrangle the girls and Shadow and maneuver them out the front doors of the community center. The sun is low in the sky as we hustle out to my 4Runner with

Shadow trotting along, tongue lolling.

Just as I locate my keys deep in my crossbody bag, I spot a figure at the edge of the lot, half-shadowed by an enormous ponderosa pine. Black hair, dark glasses, and arms knotted tight across a ribcage.

Joanne.

She's not moving, only hanging around, almost blending into the shade of the tree. If I didn't know better, I'd say she was trying to hide in the shadows. But then her eyes track the movement of the girls and my dog, and she visibly flinches when she sees me.

I hand the keys to Apple and ask for her help getting Shadow loaded into the car. Then, I make a beeline over, forcing a casual wave from her.

"Joanne! I was hoping to run into you today." I keep my voice even.

She shifts her weight, tucking her chin, and then lifting a hand in greeting. "Hi, Libby." It's just above a whisper. Her form appears smaller today, even more frail.

"You okay? You look like you saw a ghost."

She lets out a brittle laugh. "Not a ghost. Just—uh, old news." She dabs at her temple with the corner of her sleeve. "Is it warmer out than usual?"

"Want to sit in the car and cool off?" I offer, jerking my thumb at the 4Runner.

She shakes her head. "No. I … well, I am waiting for Willow. But then she texted that she's running late." There's a raspiness in her voice, or maybe she just hasn't had enough water today.

I look at her, then at the crowd still streaming in and out of the building. "You sure everything's fine?"

She tugs her sunglasses down, revealing bloodshot

eyes. "I'm not fine," she says, so quietly I barely hear. "But I'll manage. Willow, well, she thinks she can fix everything. We'll see if she can."

I sidestep so we're both in the tree's shade, and wait to see if she'll tell me more.

"She did it again," Joanne says, voice suddenly sharp. "Told me she had a 'lead' on my husband. She told me someone had seen him in Payson last week. That's not possible."

I cock my head. "Why not?"

She hesitates, a war raging behind those sunglasses. "Because he's gone, Libby. He's not coming back. I wish she'd just let it go." Her mouth twists as if she wants to say something else, but can't make herself.

I choose my words carefully. "When you say *gone*, do you mean …"

She finishes for me. "Dead? Or just disappeared? Who knows? The man was always running from something." She sniffs, then shakes her head. "Willow wants a villain, but sometimes things just fall apart."

I study her, and something about arched shoulders and hollow cheeks makes me wonder if there's more to the story. "Is that why you left Mississippi? To get away from him?"

She slides the glasses back up on her nose. "It wasn't like that." But the line comes too quickly. "Look, I know you're just trying to help, but I don't need another amateur detective following me around. I've got one sister; that's already enough."

Backing off, I offer, "I'm not here to meddle. Just—if you need anything, or want to talk, I'm around." I wave my phone. "Anytime."

She gives a brief nod, then stares at the row of cars like they might all roll away at once and leave her stranded.

I let the quiet stretch, then try again. "Oh, the reason I was looking for you earlier in the day was to see if you got my message? Would you like to do it sooner—"

"Because you're not busy enough?" She looks up finally, and I see the edge of a smirk.

I can't help but laugh.

She relaxes a hair, then wipes at her cheek. "Sorry. My anxiety has made me snippy lately."

"I get it." I nod, watching the twins bicker over who gets shotgun, and for a moment the universe feels like it's suspended. "We're headed to the charity ball, so we've gotta go get all dolled up. I should get back to them. Are you going? Is Willow going?"

She considers, then shakes her head. "Nah, not my thing. I'm not sure whether she is going." Her fingers tighten around her phone, the knuckles stark against her skin. "I hope so. I could use a night on my own. She's relentless, you know."

"Sisters are like that."

She nods once more, and I sense she's about to share more when a thud and a yelp from across the lot break the spell.

A teenage boy—six-three, or taller, in a battered football jersey—stumbles backward from behind the SUV parked next to mine. He looks around, then pinpoints Joanne and me watching him.

For a second, he flashes a sheepish grin and pretends to retie his shoe. It's one of the helpers from the volunteer day, I realize. The kid who'd helped move the sculpture crate. He straightens up, wipes sweat from his brow, and says, "Ma'am," to Joanne as if he's being graded.

Joanne stares at him for a second too long. He gives a brief salute and ambles away, but not before shooting her another glance over his shoulder.

I file the interaction away, and I decide to use levity. "Who's your admirer?"

Joanne shakes her head; eyes locked on the spot where he'd stood. "No one," she murmurs. Then, almost too soft to hear, "No one at all."

Before I can press further, she steps out of the shade and heads for the sidewalk, shoes crunching the gravel, posture wound tight as a clock. She doesn't look back.

Shadow watches her go, then nudges my knee with her nose, as if to say: Let's get out of here before anything else weird happens.

I agree. But as I buckle my seatbelt and pull out onto the main road, I keep seeing the look Joanne and the kid had exchanged. Not the look of strangers. The look of people who shared a secret.

Or maybe that's only the effect this place now has on me. Everything is a mystery until it's not.

The drive home is one long, sticky-handed recounting of every moment from the festival. Annie is still exhilarated from the firefighter dance-off that I wish Willow hadn't taken her to. Apple fills us in on endless stories of how 'old people' don't know their smartphones at all—"there ought to be senior classes for these things." Shadow dozes with her chin on the center console, the picture of a dog who's lived an entire lifetime in a day.

By the time we pull into the driveway, the twins are already arguing about who gets the first shower. I settle it the way only an aunt can: "First one to the front door!

Winner gets to pick the first song for our pre-party playlist." This turns the race up to the front door into something just shy of an Olympic event, with Shadow sprinting ahead of all of us.

Inside, Greg has lined up a pair of pizzas on the kitchen counter and set out sodas and sparkling water like he's expecting a small youth group, not a pair of tween girls and their chaperone. He gives me a long, sympathetic look as I drop my purse on the table.

"You look …" he says, popping open a can of seltzer for me.

"Exhausted is the word you're looking for," I reply, with a grin.

He leans in, lowering his voice. "You want to bail out on the ball tonight? I can fake an injury."

"Not a chance." I glance at the closed bathroom door, from which comes the unmistakable wail of Annie's Broadway vibrato. "I promised these girls a real Cinderella moment."

Greg gives a two-finger salute and goes to fill Shadow's food bowl. "Let me know if you need a fairy godmother," he calls.

For the next hour, our house becomes a flurry of wet towels, curling wands, and last-minute drama. Apple asks to borrow my mascara, then spends ten minutes debating the consequences of clumpy lashes. Annie, having watched one YouTube tutorial, insists on doing her own "updo" and promptly gets her hair so tangled I have to cut her loose with kitchen scissors.

I manage to sneak in a five-minute shower and, while the twins debate lip gloss shades, I throw on my best attempt at grown-up elegance: black wrap dress, a pair of low-heeled black pumps, and a pair of earrings I bought in a moment of optimism but have never worn. I catch a glimpse of myself in the mirror—still a little haggard, but with cheeks flushed and eyes alive.

Downstairs, the girls appear at the top of the steps. For a second, the whole world stops: Apple in a dark blue halter neck dress, hair pulled back in a tidy ponytail; Annie in a gold chiffon number, sparkles in her hair, and a grin that could power a small city. Even Shadow seems stunned, sitting at the base of the stairs.

"Wow," I say, and I mean it. "You two look amazing."

Annie beams. "We're princesses."

Apple gives a half-smile. "Not bad for thrift shop formal wear."

Greg appears, freshly shaved and wearing an honest-to-God blazer, and whistles. "Well. Don't we clean up nice." He offers me his arm; the perfect prom date.

There's a split second before we leave, the four of us huddled by the front door, and I feel the day's worry melt away. All the weirdness—the murder, the keys, the lies and secrets and neighbor drama—it can wait.

As we step onto the porch, Annie spins in a circle, giggling. "This is the best day ever."

CHAPTER SIXTEEN

If I close my eyes, the ballroom sounds like laughter and smiles and feels like the expectation of something expensive about to happen. I can feel the nerves radiating from the rows of white folding chairs. The auction crowd always vibrates differently after sunset. The ceiling floats far above, lost in the dazzle of disco balls, each sending knifepoints of multi-colored lights skipping across the crowd.

The emcee seems perfectly suited for this job. He mounts the dais with a smoothness that makes me almost forget the week-long work that went into this event. His tuxedo fits a man who knows exactly what people want to see, and the pocket square alone likely cost more than the secondhand dress I'm wearing tonight.

"Ladies and gentlemen, friends of the Mogollon Rim, and future donors, thank you for your generosity and for wearing out your shoes on our rather substantial dance floor." He glances toward the elaborate dance space at the other end of the ballroom. The man's voice projects with a sincerity to convince folks to part with their money. There's a ripple of polite laughter. I see Beth Coggins at the corner table, lips frozen into a micro-smile.

Tonight, the main event is the silent auction. Not technically "silent" at this point, because every table is a buzzing island of whispered strategies, subtle posturing, and strolls past the bidding sheets. Each table's centerpieces are particularly lethal this year: tall vases of dyed peacock feathers that force you to dodge and weave just to make eye contact with those across the table.

The emcee stretches his arms wide, as if encompassing the entire room. "Let's begin by reminding you of what's at stake tonight!" A volunteer wheels out the first item on a cart.

In the relative hush, the emcee leans forward, lowering his tone for dramatic effect. "Our top lot tonight, courtesy of local legend Stephen Bolles: the one-of-a-kind, *ten-thousand-dollar* painting. This piece, entitled *Unity in Flight*, appeared in the *Arizona Highways* and graced the cover of *Western Contemporary*. It is both a celebration of our community and a powerful statement about transcending boundaries." He lets that phrase hang.

The next lot is a weekend retreat at a mountain cabin—"rustic luxury on the Rim, sleeps six, bring your sense of adventure"—and you can hear the subtle recalibration of priorities in the laughter that follows. This one is the crowd-pleaser, the one everyone will bid on out of a sense of social obligation and the secret hope they'll win.

Then come the collector edition prints, signed by regional artists, and framed in reclaimed barnwood, which the emcee describes with a syrupy reverence usually reserved for wine tastings or deceased relatives.

"Each print is a unique vision of our beloved Mogollon Rim," he intones, and I stifle a giggle. A woman in a sequined pantsuit—a friend of Beth's from Sedona, if I remember right—dabs at her eyes, pretending to be moved by the story behind the prints. The art is pretty, I'll give them that, but tears? Really?

After casually passing the tables with many low-value, everyday items on them, he reveals the final showstopper is a handcrafted cedar kayak. This is the moment where the emcee really hits his stride, rolling the r's in "custom river-runner" and invoking "the legacy of the pioneering Rim settlers." There's something almost heroic about the way he paces in front of the item, hand slicing the air like a conductor's baton. I glance around and see the kayak already has a fan club—a gaggle of high schoolers, texting furiously under the table with almost religious awe.

They positioned the bidding sheets on little acrylic stands next to each item, alongside a fleet of clipboards. People make a show of pretending not to care about the outcome, but I see the same faces circling back again and again, just checking, their hands fidgeting with the pens like they're loaded weapons. This is the part that always gets exciting; the frantic last-minute run as the closing bell approaches, the sudden shoves and passive-aggressive side-eyes.

The emcee, now at peak performance, weaves through the tables. "Place your bids now, folks; you're helping the Rim's firefighters!" His assistant follows a half-step behind, reminding guests to "be sure to write your contact information legibly."

The lights shift—one of Beth's volunteers, maybe, or the janitor moonlighting as a stagehand. It's subtle, but the overheads fade, and the auction items themselves flare brighter, as those halogens highlight the strategically placed coveted items. The emcee checks his watch, milking the tension.

"Final bids, please!" His voice cuts through the air, and for a few seconds, the only sound is the muffled conversations amongst the tables.

The emcee straightens his jacket, flashes the crowd with his smile, and declares, "We'll reveal the winners before the end of the evening—don't go anywhere!" There's a storm of applause, then the man hands the podium back to no one in particular, and vanishes behind the curtain.

I let myself sink against our table, knees buckling for just a second before I remember I'm supposed to be an ambassador for tonight's "healing services" raffle basket. My calves ache already, and I haven't even made the rounds yet.

On the other side of the room, Beth Coggins is already prepping for the next round. She catches my eye, offers a brief nod—equal parts thanks and "don't you dare screw this up"—and disappears into the crowd. I wonder how many of them know that tonight's event is keeping the volunteer firefighters afloat for one more year, and the community center able to bring the towns together like this. Or maybe they do, and that's the thrill.

I turn toward the dance floor to see the teens whooping it up. Apple and Annie are at the center of the group, their blonde ponytails in perfect rhythm. They've only been in town for a couple days, but already there's something about the way Apple's chin tilts with cautious calculation, or the excitement in Annie's gestures.

The DJ—brought in from Show Low and old enough to have been someone's substitute teacher—is mixing late-nineties pop into modern viral hits, which seems to satisfy both the kids and their bored chaperones. The bass thuds hard enough to shake the punch bowl, but the music never gets raunchy enough for anyone to be offended. At the edge of the floor, clusters of parents and older siblings pretend not to watch their charges. I recognize more than a few of the high school boys from our volunteer work, awkward and desperate to be cool. That reminds me of the interaction Joanne had earlier. Was I mistaken, or were there flirtatious vibes? Ew.

Greg drifts to my side, two plastic champagne flutes in hand, and nods toward the fray. "They look happy."

"They do, don't they?" I say, continuing to keep a close eye on them and remembering what Jordan had said about them being boy-crazy.

He nudges me gently with his elbow, passing over a flute. "You know they're probably safer here than they are at home. Everyone's watching. Some of these parents are ex-military. The twins are fine."

I take a sip and let the bubbly soda fizz up my sinuses. "Apple's just … she doesn't always read people the right way, you know? She'll assume someone's flirting is a geometry puzzle."

"And Annie?"

"She'll egg on those boys just to watch them sweat."

Greg's mouth quirks at the edges, the faintest of laughs escaping. "Like mother, like daughter."

I elbow him back. "I'm not sure she was ever that brave." Remembering how quiet my sister was back then when she was their age.

He sets his flute aside and reaches for my hand. "Come on. We have a window. Let's act like adults for a change."

With no opportunity to protest, Greg's grip is warm and certain. The center of the floor cleared as the DJ dropped something retro enough to chase the high schoolers to the sidelines. The adults—mostly board members, a few visiting dignitaries, and the requisite county supervisor—take to the wood in a careful shuffle, trying not to spill drinks or tip over the centerpiece arrangements on their way over.

Greg is a surprisingly graceful dancer. Not that I should be surprised—he has the posture of a man who spends a lot of time working out and building those muscles. He doesn't say much, just moves, guiding me through the steps without showing off or making it a performance. It's so easy that, after a minute, I stop worrying about who's watching us and just let myself ride the music. Thinking of our upcoming wedding, I float around in circles imagining this being the night.

Across the dance floor, I spot Beth and Taz. Beth's hair has come loose from its braid and swings with every turn; her face is open and soft in a way I haven't seen before. Taz is shorter than her by half a foot but leads with surprising authority, her head thrown back as she shouts-laughs the lyrics to the power ballad. The two of them move like they've done this a hundred times, and maybe they have— how many fundraisers, how many end-of-summer balls?

I glance over his shoulder, searching for the twins. I spot them near the punch table, Annie and Apple holding court with a mix of giddy girls and stammering boys. Annie is pantomiming an elaborate story, Apple listening with that unreadable, slightly condescending half-smile she gets. Both of them look healthy. Present.

The DJ switches gears again, cueing up a country two-step, and the entire flavor of the room shifts. Couples rearrange, kids cluster by the snack tables, and the older folks—mostly ranchers and their wives—swagger onto the floor with practiced confidence. I try to pull away, but Greg just tightens his hold.

"Relax," he says. "If you trip, I'll take the blame."

So I follow his lead, even though I have no idea what I'm doing. The steps are easy enough; it's the letting-go that's tricky. My feet want to anticipate every move, but Greg just laughs and slows down, letting the rest of the world blur past us.

For a moment, the entire fundraiser becomes a single moving organism, every part joined by a ridiculous sense of momentum. I'm sweating and laughing and almost forget that I'm also supposed to be on duty.

CHAPTER SEVENTEEN

I'm searching the room for the twins when I feel a distinctive shift in the building's mood. Maybe it's the sudden gust of cold air from the vestibule, or the faint, familiar rumble of a laugh I don't recognize. I crane my neck and spot Ted Bolton at the main doors, his frame blotting out half the light in the entryway, a silhouette in flannel and sheepskin that dwarfs even the garishly oversized welcome sign.

Ted waves in our direction. Tonight, he radiates a strange, manic good cheer that draws eyes and elbows from every table he passes. He looks freshly scrubbed, the wild curls tamed, cheeks pink from the night air or maybe the prospect of an open bar. I watch him cross the room, greeting old friends with a backslap, a joke, a word I can't lip-read but am certain is jovial.

He's halfway to the auction table when he's intercepted by a group of retired locals, their faces craggy and battered. He's laughing, palms up in surrender as the old guard busts his chops about the beard, the new truck, and his recent dust-ups in town. Ted absorbs it all with a kind of bruised humility, never letting the smile slip. Maybe that's his secret: he knows how to take a punch.

Greg drifts in behind me, eyes following Ted's progress. "He looks good," he says. Not a compliment, just an observation.

"Give it an hour," I whisper, still unsure about the man I unexpectedly discovered on our property and who punched a guy at the local eatery earlier this week.

The double doors swing open again, and Willow Springs enters, half-shadowed by the floral arch and at least a head taller than her companion. The companion is Joanne, hair ironed straight and glossy, lipstick darker than I've seen her wear, a dress that's too chic for this room, but somehow fits her like a second skin. For a heartbeat, I don't recognize her. I certainly hadn't expected her to be here.

Beth must have given them the head table by the stage, because that's where Willow steers Joanne, nodding greetings to those in their path. As a first, Joanne's sunglasses are nowhere in sight—her eyes are wide, a little wild, taking in the disco balls, the auction items, and the sprawl of unfamiliar faces. If she's nervous, she's hiding it with a rigid, queenly posture. I move toward her, but Greg gently grabs my wrist, just enough to slow me down.

"Let them land first," he murmurs.

So, I watch. Ted, still the center of attention at the

firefighters' table, glances up and spots Joanne. The effect is immediate: his smile falters, his face opens, and for a split second, I see actual, unguarded hope. He breaks from the man-pack and angles toward her; his hands jammed in his pockets like he's rehearsing what to do with them. The collision is gentle but seismic—a soft handshake, a word from Joanne, then a shared laugh. No show, no bravado.

Willow is less amused. She hovers nearby, arms crossed, scanning the perimeter. Her gaze rakes over me and Greg, then slides back to Joanne, as if waiting for the first sign of distress. There's history there, obviously. From what I'd already learned, it's clearly more than I'll ever know.

I risk a quick approach, keeping my posture loose and nonthreatening, like I'm wandering toward the snacks rather than running interference.

"Hey, stranger," I say, aiming for casual.

Joanne looks up, and something like gratitude flickers in her eyes. "Hi, Libby. Didn't think I'd see you here."

"I could say the same," I tease, wondering if she truly forgot how I'd asked her to come with us. "Thought you were avoiding these things."

She shrugs, a gesture so small I almost miss it. "Willow thought it would be good."

I glance at Willow, who's busy chatting up a volunteer but definitely listening with one ear.

"I'm glad you came," I say, and mean it. "You look great."

Joanne ducks her head, embarrassed.

Ted chooses this moment, armed with three tiny glasses of champagne. He hands one to Joanne and one to Willow, then raises his own in a toast. "To beautiful women who make this place worth living in," he booms, earning a round of nervous laughter from the nearest table. He winks at Joanne, and the two of them touch glasses with a satisfying plastic clink. I catch Willow's scoff right before she sips.

It's weird watching them together. Ted is gentler than I've ever seen, deferential but not pathetic, like he knows how close he came to missing this chance. Joanne, for her part, seems almost lighter, her careful edges softening in Ted's presence. I remember her telling me how she hates parties—how they remind her of what she'd lost. Tonight, she looks like she's finally taking something back.

Greg joins us. "I see you two have met," he says, addressing Joanne directly. "Ted's a good guy."

She nods, visibly relieved. Willow edges closer, hand on the small of Joanne's back, and for a second, I brace for impact. But the sisters exchange a silent, wary truce.

The music swells, and Ted makes an awkward show of inviting Joanne to dance. She hesitates, then accepts, glancing over her shoulder at Willow. They step onto the floor together, two shapes silhouetted against the whirling lights.

I stand with Greg and Willow, watching the crowd. "You knew she'd come," I say quietly.

Willow doesn't look at me. "I hoped," she says. "She needs it more than she admits."

The next song is a slow one, and Ted and Joanne move in close, heads bowed, lost in their own conversation.

Greg squeezes my hand. "You want to dance?"

I shake my head, content to watch, at least for now. "I'm good," I say. "I want to remember this."

Then, I notice the mood shifts as Joanne returns to her table. A woman I don't know, done up in a fuchsia pantsuit that could blind someone from a hundred yards away, sidles up to the table with a plastic flute in hand. Whatever is said between them, only they know.

The air tightens. Joanne freezes, lips parted in a half-smile that doesn't quite fit. There's obvious tension between the two, and I wonder if I should step in to make sure Joanne is okay. Before I can get my feet moving in her direction, Joanne clutches the front of her dress, a blooming red Rorschach stain across her torso. For a moment, she just stands there, blinking, as if waiting for someone to reset the scene.

She pivots on one foot and bolts for the double doors, heels clattering against the floor with every step. The room's attention seems to follow her, then shifts to Willow, whose face goes a shade paler than the tablecloths.

Greg, in the middle of a dance with Beth, stops short. He mutters something to her, then cuts across the floor, collecting Ted in his wake. I follow at a distance, not sure if I'm needed or just morbidly curious.

They find Joanne in the hallway, pressed against a column, breathing hard. Ted is the first to reach her, his voice a low rumble. "Joanne, you okay?"

She shakes her head once, sharp and birdlike. "That… that woman…" Her hands flutter at her sides, smearing red into the silk. "Oh, it's fine; I'm fine. I just—need a minute."

Greg steps in, tone gentle but insistent. "Joanne, are you hurt?"

I rush to her side.

Joanne's look is one of bewilderment. "It's just wine, guys!"

Ted glances at me, then back at Greg, shaking his head. Beth and Willow join our gathering in the hallway.

Joanne regains her composure first. She straightens, dabs at her dress, and offers a brittle smile. "Sorry for the scene. I just hate red wine—look at the mess it's made."

Ted cracks a smile. "You should've stuck with champagne."

She rolls her eyes. The tension dissolves, if only a little. Greg gives Ted a nod, like a quarterback calling a play, and Ted steers Joanne toward the restroom. Willow watches them go, her face a mask of something between worry and resentment.

Greg asks her, "Who was that woman talking to Joanne?"

She shrugs. "I don't know. Have you seen her around, Libby?"

"No, but their conversation was contentious from what I could see."

The ballroom hums on, and I peek inside to see that Apple and Annie are back on the dance floor. I don't spot the fuchsia woman anywhere.

After the drama with Joanne, the rest of the night has a dreamlike, muted quality—everyone a little softer, a little more careful. The energy dips, but nobody wants to be the first to leave, so the crowd hovers in the ballroom, sipping punch and waiting for the silent auction results.

The emcee is back in the mix and waits until the hour chimes to start the winner announcements. He ascends the dais with the poise of a politician and gestures for quiet. The crowd obliges, their curiosity outweighing their fatigue.

"First, I want to thank everyone for making this year's ball the best-attended in our history," he begins. There's polite applause, a few overeager whoops from the high schoolers. "Thanks to your generosity, we've raised over twenty thousand dollars for the Heber Fire Department, the volunteer firefighters, and our community programs."

People clap, and this time it feels genuine. He moves on to the auction results, reading from a stack of color-coded envelopes. The lesser lots go first: numerous gift baskets, tea sets, gift cards for local businesses, the weekend cabin, the kayak, the collector's prints. Winners are called by name, each making their way to the front, offering hugs and handshakes. The real suspense hangs over the top prize—the Stephen Bolles' painting.

Our emcee draws out the moment, his pause almost theatrical. "And now, for our final lot: *Unity in Flight*. The winning bidder is…"

He glances at the card, eyebrows lifting a fraction. "Patty Baumgarten!"

There's a scattering of applause, but mostly everyone's heads are twisting back and forth, waiting for whoever Patty is to come forward. No one does.

"Patty must have left, but we're thrilled for her, and we'll deliver her painting this week."

CHAPTER EIGHTEEN

The next morning, the festival is still buzzing. They moved all activities outside, and the community center changed back to an office-like feel. Even so, as I walk straight through to the office, I see some evidence of a raucous time—wrinkled streamers on the floor, numerous filled garbage bags waiting to load into the dumpster, and Beth's leftover kombucha sweating in the corner. Alone in the office, with the relentless hum of the mini-fridge, I seem to have an over-caffeinated energy in my fingertips. I can't sit still.

I'm elbow-deep in the silent auction paperwork; three hundred separate receipts and still four items unclaimed. I look up from the desk—the *Unity in Flight* painting is propped up in the corner, boxed up and ready for delivery, but the petty cash box doesn't match the ledger.

It's while cross-referencing the physical donation forms with Beth's color-coded spreadsheet that I find the first crumb. Actually, Shadow finds it—sort of. She pounces with her front paws on my lap, twisting her body in excitement, her tail swishing the papers everywhere.

"Sweet girl, not now. Maybe in a little while we'll walk around the grounds. Apple and Annie are out there somewhere."

She backs down as I gather everything from the floor. Picking up several loose papers, I see a couple of smudged signatures—one belonging to a local restaurant manager, the other in tight mechanical script, "P. Sanchez." Next to it is a notation: "for coin rolls; see storage." The scrawl, which looks like it was written in a moving car, has no contact number or address.

I flip back to the auction summary, confused because I was sure this referenced the coins that I never picked up. *When had they arrived at the center? Who delivered them?* Seemed too coincidental.

There's an entry on Beth's spreadsheet related to rolls of state quarters. Delving deeper into the notes, I discovered that nobody bid on the bucket of state quarters in Lot 6, or they never included them in the silent auction, and I wasn't sure which. I see a bucket under the coffee table and get up to see what's in it. The sticky note on the bucket says: "Kids Area—DO NOT COUNT."

Curious whether the donor left a voice message that might still be in the system, I dial the center's voicemail. Skipping through a dozen hang-ups and two telemarketers, I hear a man's deep-throated voice: "This is Paul Sanchez. I donated a few items for the fundraiser, including some coins—uncirculated, state commemorative. If there's any trouble with the authenticity, please reach me at—" The call cuts off there, almost like he changed his mind about leaving a number.

I write "Paul Sanchez = coins" in block letters at the top of my notepad and underline it three times. Now for the first time, I have the man's first name. It has to be the same person I was supposed to meet in Show Low.

I decide to hit Beth up for answers before my brain ties itself into a full-body knot. She's at the prep table in the main hall, sleeves rolled to her elbows, hair pinned back with a couple of decorative oriental sticks. The table is a disaster zone—boxes, packing tape, and drifting feathers from last night's centerpieces. Beth is methodically stacking plates to be packed away, her face a serene mask of "I have this under control."

"Morning," I say. "Hope you're up for round two."

She doesn't look up. "Been up since 4 a.m. You want some caffeine? I think the Keurig is still alive."

"I'm good. But I have a question." I wave the paperwork like a crime scene photo. "Since I never picked up the coins, I'm confused as to why they're sitting under the coffee table in the office. Can you tell me when they were delivered? Who brought them in?"

Beth stops stacking, finally makes eye contact. Her expression is bland, but her mouth does a brief twitch that means she's been caught off guard. "I think it was that same guy, if I recall correctly. Why?"

I stare for a moment. "Any explanation for why I was sent on a wild goose chase then? Also, I don't recall those being offered in the silent auction last night."

Slowly shaking her head, she answers, "I'm not sure they were."

"Well, he left a voice message about authenticity. Like he expects someone to challenge the coins. Maybe there was a problem with them, and that's why they were held back from the auction?"

She shrugs, defaulting to nonchalance. "Not that I know of. I handed them to Mrs. Wren for the kids' area and figured they'd end up as bingo prizes down the road."

I tap my pen against the table. "But, Beth … don't you think the police should question him about his role in—well, the *murder*? Do you really think it was a coincidence?"

Beth's patience is legendary, but it's not infinite. She draws a deep, cleansing breath. "Libby, not everyone in this town has an agenda. I'm sure the police have already figured that out—it's none of your business."

How many times have I been told that in my life? "I know. But I have a feeling about …."

"It seems you have a feeling about everyone." She sips her kombucha.

"Sometimes I'm right."

She shakes her head, then softens. "I'll pull his donor form from the file. If you want to chase him down, be my guest. But please, for my sanity, don't get the center involved in a 'coin conspiracy.' Not this week."

I promise nothing, then head back to the office and straight to the bucket still sitting under the coffee table. Sitting on the couch, I rifle through, pulling out the coin rolls. Each one has a band of masking tape sealing it, which is marked with a state and year.

I snap a picture and text it to Greg: Remember those coins I went to pick up? Well, I found them.

He replies three minutes later with question marks and a confused face emoji. Libby, be careful.

Be careful … Probably should be the Madsen family motto.

I stare at the coins for a few more seconds before returning to the paperwork. The rest of the morning blurs past. I chase down auction winners, schedule deliveries, and field an incoming call from an elderly woman who wants to know if she can return a signed baseball "if it's cursed." Beth flags me down before lunch and hands over a single sheet from the donor files: "Sanchez, Paul. See also: 'Collector,' 'Appraiser,' and 'Authentication.' Formerly Phoenix."

A quick Google search gives me a headshot—the kind you'd see in a faculty directory. Narrow face, hawk nose, dark hair going silver at the temples. There's a string of old interviews with Arizona news outlets, mostly about estate sales and the authenticity of lost treasures. One article links him to a controversy over counterfeit coins in Tempe, but nothing ever came of it. A few clicks deeper, and the trail runs cold. The last public mention was five years old.

I stew over this for another hour while also finishing up volunteer work in the office, then decide there's only one person who'll know if there's a bigger story here. It's time to visit the police and hand over what I know. Maybe the twins would like to take a drive over to Show Low first thing Monday morning?

Then I remembered how Beth had asked me to deliver that painting as soon as Patty paid for it, so I relaxed and joined the girls outside instead. These things can wait; there's no need for two separate trips to Show Low.

I find Apple and Annie happily working their stations: Annie helping a group of kiddos with the goldfish game, and today Apple joined another teen girl selling lemonade.

Before I approach, Willow swoops in.

"There you are! I've been looking all over." She threads her arm through my elbow and walks along with me, but only after giving Shadow her greeting, too.

"Did you have fun last night?" I asked.

"Wasn't it spectacular?" she says, dreamily looking to the sky.

I agree and comment on how long it'd been since I'd danced.

"I'm worried about Joanne, though," she whispers.

"How so?"

"Well, you saw her reaction with the spilled wine. Don't you think she overreacted?"

"What did she say about it when you guys left?"

"She didn't. Shut me out entirely and then closed herself off in her room."

I really don't care to get involved in the sisters' spat, so I try diversion instead. "She and Ted seemed to hit it off."

Shadow barks, looking up at me.

Willow scoffs. "Yeah, and she's still married!" We both look down at Shadow when she barks yet again, almost as if she had something to add to the conversation.

"Oh, now you're concerned about that? I thought you were encouraging her to get out?"

She hangs her head. "I'm not sure what to believe. She hardly talks to me at all about her life. I mean, she called me weeks back, upset and crying. I thought I was helping by offering her a place to stay, even if only for a little while. But since she arrived here, I'm reconsidering."

"Are things that bad between you two?"

"I hardly know her anymore. Back when we were kids, we were tight. Now, there's a huge, thick wall between us, and I don't understand why."

I remember a few things Joanne shared with me and offer a suggestion. "Maybe don't try so hard? Just relax and see how things unfold. Worrying won't get you anywhere."

She lets go of my arm and stops. "Sometimes I think she's hiding much bigger problems. How am I supposed to help her if she won't confide in me?"

Shadow sits on her foot, rubbing her face along her jeans. Willow reaches down and pets her.

Smiling at the two of them, I simply offer, "You can't. She has to be ready, and when she is, you also have to be ready to receive whatever she confides." I reach out and touch her arm. "Relax. Things will work out in their own time."

She gives me a half-smile. "What is your volunteer assignment today?"

"Well, I helped in the office all morning. And now I'm looking for Beth to determine how much longer the girls will be working. I kinda wanted to get them out of here and do something different with our afternoon."

"What are you thinking?"

"Maybe take a drive? Or, go for a hike. It feels like since they arrived, this is all we've been doing."

She nods. "Is Greg working today?"

"Yes—seems like every day." I smile widely. "Hey! Why don't we all get together this evening and grill something? You and Joanne—and whoever else. Maybe Ted would like to join?" I tease.

"That sounds fun. I'll suggest it to Joanne, but no promises."

We agree she'll call me later, and then we go our separate ways. I look around the grounds for the harried woman carrying a clipboard, but don't see her, so I pull out my phone and dial Greg. He doesn't answer, so I quickly type out a message asking if he'd like to have company over for dinner.

When I look up again, I spy Beth emerging from the community center, so Shadow and I chase after her.

Soon enough, Shadow and the twins are loaded into my 4Runner, ready to get some lunch and go hike to a pond not far away from the house. Before we lose cell signal, I see Greg answered my text, readily agreeing to the dinner plans, saying he'd invite Ted. I text Willow, giving her the plan. Something told me that Ted would convince Joanne to join in.

After our hike, and by the time we pulled into our driveway, Greg was already home. He greeted us and helped carry in the grocery bags filled with goodies for the evening.

"Ted joining us?" I asked.

"Yep. Said he'll never turn down free food."

I set the bags on the kitchen counter and then turn to give my fiancé an enormous hug and kiss. "I've missed you today! And I was telling Willow earlier how much I loved dancing with you last night. Can't wait for our wedding reception!"

"Speaking of which, I found a local country-western band that was affordable. Recommendation from one of the guys at work. What do you think?"

"Anything that doesn't involve one more task for me— I'm all for it!" I tip-toed again and planted a kiss on his lips.

Apple groans. "Get a room…"

We chuckle at her exaggerated disgust. The twins help me marinate chicken, mix a dry rub for the London broil, and wash and chop vegetables.

"What do you think—a pan of brownies or fresh-baked cookies?"

Annie pipes up, "Let's do cookies but make ice cream sandwiches with the ice cream we still have from the other night."

"Oooh, I like your thinking."

The girls mix the ingredients and take charge of the cookie baking. Seeing they had everything under control, I take a moment for myself and head to the bedroom.

The evening turns out lovely—a relaxed mix of conversation, playfulness with Shadow and the girls, and it appears we also brought Joanne out of her shell by playing some games. She seemed much more relaxed around her sister, but I saw Willow keeping a watchful eye on her, especially every time Joanne and Ted walked away from the group.

"She's a grown adult, Willow," I remind her.

"I know. It's just that she left home so young. Now she's back, and I don't want her disappearing again."

I notice the language she uses, and it strikes me as odd. As though Joanne ran away from *her*. Not my business, I tell myself. I sit back, enjoying my wine.

Greg stokes the fire in the pit. We all gather around as the evening cools enough that several of us also put sweaters on.

In a private moment, I ask Joanne, "Who was that lady you were talking to at the dance last night? Her eyes searched mine questioningly.

"When the wine got spilled on you?"

"Oh! The lady who *tossed* her wine on me? Mistaken identity, I guess."

"How so?"

"I don't know who she is, but she lit into me as though I'd just slept with her husband."

"Is that what she accused you of?"

"Not exactly. I don't know what she was going on about. Crazy for sure."

I sit back in my chair, remembering what I'd witnessed. It sure appeared to me, from across the room, that they knew each other. I decide not to press the subject now; Joanne has no reason to lie to me, so I accept her answer.

Ted and Greg get up and head into the house for more beer. Willow and the girls are deep in conversation.

"Looks like you and Ted hit it off last night…" I tease Joanne.

"Oh, c'mon." She blushes. "He's a good guy, isn't he?"

"I don't know him well, but Greg swears so."

"Good looking too … in that teddy bear sort of way."

I chuckle at the imagery. He's a giant teddy bear, except when he's lurking around on the property or getting in a bar fight. That thought sits with me as particularly unsettling, even when I convince myself and rationalize that he's only been on the property to do a job, to help us. What was it about Ted that caused this anxiety in me?

CHAPTER NINETEEN

The Show Low police station is about forty-five minutes from home. By the time I pull in, the parking lot is already half full of government vehicles, SUVs and trucks. The building is newer than the rest of town—wood siding, metal roof. I hadn't noticed that detail the last time I was here. Inside, the air conditioning is set to arctic, and another thing I never noticed before, the waiting area is decorated with a mural of smiling kids holding hands with uniformed officers. Nobody at the counter this morning, just a tarnished service bell and a sign-in sheet.

I scrawl my name and stand awkwardly until a deputy in khakis ambles out from the back. I recognize him instantly. His badge says Chesky.

He takes one look at me and cracks up. "Libby! Causing

trouble again?"

I smile, not sure if it's a compliment. "Only good trouble. Can I ask you something? Off the record?"

He waves me to follow him. The bullpen is a haphazard arrangement of mismatched desks and aging computers; obviously, they spent the budget on the building but not on the interior or on upgrading the technology. Chesky motions for me to sit, then props himself on a short filing cabinet.

"What's up?"

I slide my notepad across the desk. "Do you know a Paul Sanchez? I've learned that this might be the man I was supposed to pick up coins from."

He whistles, impressed. "Going big, huh? Didn't think you'd go full private-eye on us."

I suppress the urge to fidget. "I've found some things during my work at the community center—remember, I told you I was volunteering there. Apparently, we got that donation from him, but this shows that it arrived at the community center *after* the last time I was here."

He moves to a desk and starts typing, hen-pecking with one finger at each key. After a minute, he leans back. "Sanchez, Paul. No criminal, but lots of civil complaints. And look at this—coin collecting; looks like some claims were related to that."

"I don't understand … like, for what?"

Chesky scrolls. "Property. Art and coin collectibles. Was once involved in an estate fraud case, but nothing stuck. Sued a guy named Spiegel—totally unrelated to coins though, and looks like it's sealed."

I jolt. "Spiegel?"

Chesky shrugs. "Why?"

"The address where I found that dead body. Wasn't the

homeowner Martin Spiegel? Are we talking about the same person? Isn't that suspicious?"

He leans in, suddenly serious. "Doesn't mean it's related. Listen, Libby, we're already investigating that homicide. Don't get involved."

"Okay."

He laughs. "You're a terrible liar, Madsen. Anything else I can pull for you?"

I consider, then go for broke. "Have you learned anything further about the identity of the deceased? Because I might have more for you there as well."

"You have already been snooping around!" he glares, but then a smile breaks out and I relax.

"No, really. They find me."

"Uh, huh," he teases.

"I ran into a neighbor lady, and she said a friend of Marty's had been around his place for several months prior to his death. She wasn't sure whether he was actually staying there, but he was there often."

"Yes, we know about that."

"Okay, good. But also, I learned that they'd been friends dating back to grade school."

"Okay? And?"

"Well, maybe there's something to it?"

"We haven't been able to talk to Martin Spiegel yet. We're working on it." He clears his throat, turning his head toward a pile of manila folders on his desk. He pulls one out, opens it and thumbs through the papers.

When he looks up, I smile, hoping he'll share more. "Listen, we can help each other. You know I had nothing to do with the murder, but there's something about the man found there and whoever murdered him. They must have been personally involved."

"How so?"

"Stabbing ... seems personal."

He nods, then stares again at his notes in the folder. He grunts as he slides the folder across the desk, and I stop it with my hand.

Opening it, I see the report is as bare-bones as it gets: Paul Sanchez's last known address, a handwritten note about a "domestic dispute," and a single-page incident summary. No mention of questioning neighbors, but there's a reference to another property on Pinedale Road, and a name scrawled in blue ink off in the margin: "Marty Spiegel".

"So, you are on to him as a suspect?"

Chesky frowns. "Person of interest, mainly because the deceased was found in his home. But if he's mixed up with Sanchez, or these collectibles, it's probably about money."

"Okay, so what do we know about Marty Spiegel?"

His side-eye glance makes me recoil. "*We* know that he's an insurance adjuster. He's lived on the Mogollon Rim for most of his adult life. We're trying to learn more about where he came from before that, because we know he wasn't born in Arizona. That's all I'm comfortable sharing right now."

"And anything further about the deceased—I think I was told the last name was Blankenship."

"Nothing yet. But seriously, Libby, leave this up to us. No snooping around."

I thank him, then drive home with my brain running wild. Sanchez, Spiegel, and Blankenship—three men orbiting the same patch of high country, each possibly with their own potential shadowed history.

I park in our driveway, staring out, wondering how the girls' day with Shadow and Greg went, until the sun glances off the windshield and makes me squint. He took them hiking and promised it wouldn't be too strenuous. As I procrastinate going inside, my mind wanders back to the conversation with Officer Chesky. Surprised he shared as much as he did, I think of all the information I now know. I want to believe it's just a puzzle, that the edges will fit together if I push hard enough. But somewhere behind my eyes, a voice like Beth's whispers: Not everyone in this town has an agenda.

No, I'm not convinced.

CHAPTER TWENTY

I learned through my own massage therapy licensing that it takes less than thirty seconds to check someone's certification history in the state of Arizona. The licensing bureau posts the entire thing online—plumbing, hairdressing, even the people who install home security systems. So, it's only natural, after realizing how slow law enforcement is, that I must scour the web for any mechanic with the last name Blankenship. That neighbor lady had mentioned the guy was good with cars—it might be a shot in the dark, but I had to try.

The result pops up on the first page. There's a badge-sized headshot: a sunburned man with a chinstrap beard. "Blankenship, Russell M.," it says. Licensed in automotive repair, issued years back though. No idea if this is the guy.

I click through, hoping for an address, but the only extra data is a line about "self-employed, mobile service calls only." There's no mugshot, no glaring criminal record, just the achievement of a life spent under the hood. But what gets me is the date of birth: same year as Greg. That means this Russ was just over forty, which means it could be him.

Wait a minute. Another coincidence? Joanne's husband's name is Russ, isn't it? Was that what she'd told me when reliving her history with him—had she said his name? Even with the little-known backstory, this now sits in my brain like a splinter. Had I ever even asked what he did for a living—maybe this is a total coincidence? Did I even know her last name? My brain was fuzzy.

I push away from my laptop and stretch my arms overhead, feeling the vertebrae pop like bubble wrap. The sun is cresting the line of pines, and the clock says it's not even 7:30 a.m., but my heart is already racing like I'm late for an exam. I'm not, but I might as well be: today is the big day, the center's post-fundraiser clean-up and then a strategy meeting for the next event. No one was more surprised than me when Beth asked me to be there.

The girls are slow to rise this morning, and I am fine with letting them sleep in. They've been superstar workers for days now, so they deserve to lounge around. Willow offered to take them to the lake today to go paddle boarding, but that won't be until afternoon when it warms up more. I am holding out hope that we'll finish the meeting so that maybe I can join them.

The community center is much quieter this morning when I walk inside. The warm smell of coffee, the yeastiness of warm bagels, fills my senses. Beth is already inside, hunched over a table with a marker-stained clipboard. She wears a look of concentration, lips moving silently as she plans her attack. I hesitate at the door, watching her for a minute, before she glances up.

"Hey," I say, trying to keep my voice neutral. "Did you even go home last night?"

She gives a lopsided smile. "I wanted to get a jump on things."

There's a flutter of paper as I set my bag down. "I need a quick favor, actually. Do you still have access to the volunteer rosters?"

She raises an eyebrow. "For what? You know most of the regulars."

"I'm looking for someone who might've gone by a different last name." I try to make it sound casual, but my voice betrays the anxiety underneath.

Beth taps a password into the center's battered desktop, then swivels the monitor so I can see. "Knock yourself out."

It takes about five minutes and a few filter settings, but I find what I'm after: near the bottom of page three, there's a "Blankenship, Joanne," listed as a part-time volunteer for the firefighter charity event we just finished. Her phone number is missing, replaced with "see Willow" in parentheses. There's also a note: "referred by sister."

I stare at the screen, mouth gone dry. I must have made a sound, because Beth edges closer.

"What?" she asks.

I point at the entry. "Willow never told me Joanne's last name."

Beth blinks, but urges me to go on. "Why? What does that matter?"

"Um," my words stick in my mouth like glue. "He's, uh, the one I found dead in Pinetop-Lakeside."

Her face turns ghostly pale.

"Do they know this?"

"That's the thing. I don't think so. And I can't be sure they're related—so please don't say anything. How long until we get started? I need to call Willow."

"You have time." She shoos me away.

I walk into one of the empty offices and close the door. Willow answers on the first ring. "Ah, ha! You bailed on work and you're going to join us today, right?"

"Uh, no. Not exactly, Willow."

"Oh, you sound serious. What's going on?"

"What's Joanne's husband's name?" I directly ask her.

There was a long pause. "What? Why?"

"Curious. Is it Blankenship?"

The silence says it all. "Again, why?"

"Remember when I was telling you about the crime scene—the one in Pinetop, you got silent when I mentioned some names. Why didn't you tell me then Russ was her husband?"

She stammers for too long. "Well, technically, he's not. At least I'm pretty sure he's not anymore. Listen, Libby … how do you…?"

"I don't. But you were concerned about it that day I mentioned it, weren't you?"

"Okay, hearing that name, yes, it startled me. But I'm sure it's a coincidence; otherwise, the police would have contacted her, wouldn't they?"

"Other than the wallet found at the scene with Russ Blankenship's driver's license in it, there isn't any other proof it was actually him. The police said they're waiting on tests to confirm identity."

"Oh boy. You don't understand, Libby. Why can't you leave this alone?" She lets out a huge sigh. "I have wanted to talk to her about his disappearance, but I haven't because I don't want him anywhere near her. He's bad news, Libby. I keep hoping she'd forget all about him!"

"Because of domestic violence?" I wasn't sure where I was going, but I spewed words anyway.

That stops her cold. Even through the phone, I could imagine Willow's face is a shifting weather map: confusion, then anger, then something like hurt. "Who told you that?"

"Honestly, it was only a theory. One that I think you've now confirmed. But the police are looking into this guy's background. If you have anything, you should speak up."

Willow quiets, then lets out another sigh. "How do we know for sure?"

"We don't."

"Dammit. I swear he'll always be a thorn in our side. Jo is very discreet about her personal life with him, but I've never liked that man. And since she's been back, she's always said he's missing, or that he moved away. What if it's just that?"

I want to believe her, but something doesn't add up.

"Jo always changes the subject when I've asked about Russ. Yes, I know something is up, but what am I supposed to do about it?" She admits she wouldn't be sad if he's dead.

I chew my lip, unsure how to proceed. "Perhaps, he is no longer a problem if he is dead?"

Willow doesn't answer right away. "She said the last time she saw Russ, he was loading the car at three in the morning, wearing a cowboy hat and a dress shirt with no buttons. He said he was leaving for Vegas, maybe California."

"Do you think she'd tell us if something happened to him?"

Willow sighs. "Maybe she's protecting herself."

There's a silence that stretches so long I almost forget how to fill it.

"I just wish," Willow says finally, "that I could stop expecting Jo to be something she's not."

I nod, not only because I agree with her, but because I don't know what else to do.

She continues, "If you're right, and Russ is dead, then maybe Jo finally gets to start over. Maybe the rest doesn't matter."

I try to imagine what that kind of starting over feels like—how you even begin. "How do we tell her?"

Willow goes silent. I realize she needs Joanne to be okay. Maybe that's the only way she can keep going, too. I wonder then how many times Joanne has tried to erase her own past. By the end of the conversation, Willow sounds defeated, and no decisions have been made. I still can't understand who killed Russ or why. I sure don't get the feeling that Joanne could have done it, but then again, I've been wrong before.

I hate having this information and I realize I should probably call Officer Chesky to report what I know. But what do I really know? And after all, I've been told more than once to stay out of their business, right?

I finish out my day with Beth and the other volunteers at the center. Willow, bless her heart, keeps her promise to take the girls to the lake. I can't imagine how difficult all this is for her.

CHAPTER TWENTY-ONE

By the time I make it out of the community center, there isn't time for me to meet up at the lake. I pull up in the driveway at home, and my pulse spikes when I see Joanne is waiting in her car. How stupid, I chastise myself. I booked her massage and had totally forgotten all about it. I glance at the clock and notice that I am only ten minutes late.

My mind keeps going back to my earlier conversation with Willow, and I decide it's best not to say anything to Joanne until Willow is with us. How I'll be able to do that, I have no idea. Maybe it's better to let Willow handle giving her the news. I take a deep breath and step out of my vehicle at the same time she does.

"Joanne! I'm so sorry I'm late. I got caught up at the

community center."

"I figured. No problem at all. I've got nothing else going on. Well, Willow kept trying to get me to join her and the girls at the lake. I didn't tell her I had a massage, but I really didn't want to go to the lake today anyway."

Guilt seeps in as I lead her toward the house.

"Hey, I've left Shadow inside all morning. Do you mind if I take her out and then we'll head over for the massage?"

"Sure!" She eagerly follows me into the house, her eyes exploring the interior as I open Shadow's kennel and let her out. "You sure do have a beautiful home, Libby."

"Thanks!" I open the back doors and let Shadow outside. Turning back to her, I add, "Well, it's Greg's place, and I'm having a hard time realizing that we're soon to be married, so it will be mine too. The whole idea of marriage…"

"What, you don't wanna?" she asks in her Southern drawl.

"Oh, no! Until I met him, I hadn't considered it. But no, of course, I'm looking forward to marrying Greg." Maybe this was my opening. "What was that like for you, if you don't mind my asking?"

"What? Marrying my husband?"

I nod and glance outside to be sure Shadow hasn't wandered too far. "Yeah, what's his name, by the way?"

Her eyes wander, admiring the grand stone fireplace in our living room, and for a couple of seconds, I think she's going to ignore my question.

"We basically eloped … there wasn't a big pronounce-ment of love, or down-on-his-knee proposal. No, none of that. So, what was it like?" She gazes into the distance, and I can almost imagine she'd placed herself amongst whatever ghosts still run wild on the banks of the Mississippi.

"It was summer, and the trees were heavy with green. Every surface sweats; the air is always thick enough to chew. I remember that well. I also remember my daddy coming unglued when he saw me talking with a boy." She stops; I see the second she lands back in the present.

"Go on… I was right there with you. Mississippi, right?"

She nods wistfully. "Well, I can tell you all about that during my massage, right?"

"Oh sure. Yes, we're losing daylight. Here, let's just go out this way and get Shadow on the way over next door." I grab the keys from the hook and step out onto the patio, calling Shadow over to us, and we all walk into the guest house.

As soon as I've scrubbed up and given Joanne enough time to disrobe and settle in on the table, I go into the room and begin her massage.

"So, you were saying that you eloped … that sounds so romantic!"

"Oh, well, at the time, I'm sure I thought that too, but trust me, it was anything but…"

Even though I can't see her face, I feel the second she steps back in time to her childhood.

"I was sixteen, or maybe just shy of my sixteenth birthday actually, standing on the back porch of my parent's house, arms wrapped around a garbage sack full of everything I owned. My hair was longer than now, jet black and slicked to my face by the humidity. I'm barefoot, toes curled over the rotten edge of the wooden steps, and *so many* mosquitoes orbiting my ankles.

"Russ waits in the shadow of a battered Oldsmobile.

He's ten years older, twice as hungry, three times as sure. He calls my name once, in that soft drawl that makes the most mundane word sound like a romantic wedding vow.

"I remember hesitating, checking the house windows behind me, but it's all dark inside. Nobody comin' to stop me, and I already made the decision—weeks ago, really, when Russ first started bringing me gifts. Cigarettes sometimes, or a bootleg tape. Once, it was a single rose from the cemetery north of town. I remember vividly: 'You deserve better,' he said, 'and I can give you that.' He made me believe it.

"That night, I just left the door unlocked, left it swinging behind me and I ran the length of the yard, sack of clothes thumping my thigh. Russ met me halfway, caught me by the wrist, and pulled me in with such strength — a man who always gets what he wants.

"We didn't even speak until we were ten miles out of town, the only light a sickle moon that kept vanishing behind torn clouds. I kept my eyes fixed on the dashboard. Russ's hands were firm on the wheel, forearms corded and tanned from years of labor. He's a large man, and I realized then he took up all the space in the car.

"I wanted to ask where we're going, but somehow knew better, or it didn't even matter. Russ only answered questions when he felt like it, and besides, the answer was always the same: 'where the money is.' That night, it was a cabin off the Natchez Trace Parkway for our first sleep."

"That's kinda romantic, isn't it?" I teased her. Immediately I felt her tense.

After another minute, she resumed.

"I don't remember exactly when I put it together that he wasn't earning money by any legal means. Well, he worked on cars and such, but most of that trip was not on the up and up. He'd prepped for weeks to go to Natchez Trace … well, some doctor's place nearby, left vacant for the summer. As he had said— 'no alarm, no dogs, easy'."

"Oh, so you didn't stay at the cabin?" I surmise.

"Well, yes, but not entirely as I expected. I remember that like yesterday. He pulled onto a dirt road, killed the headlights, and parked a ways from the cabin. He told me in an eerie whisper to wait there. 'If you see anyone, you honk twice and then run.' I was so young and naïve, I nodded, heart pounding so hard I thought it might crack my ribs. I watched as he disappeared into the trees, moving fast and with ease.

"I waited, hugging my knees and counting the seconds. Several long minutes and Russ was back, arms loaded with whatever he could carry.

"He was so proud. 'See?' he told me as he dumped the haul onto the back seat. 'Cake.'

"And, no, it wasn't literally the confectionery. I wanted to ask what was in the bag he threw in the back seat, but somehow I knew I wasn't supposed to ask more questions. The less I knew, the better. That's the rule, and I'm a quick learner. I tucked myself smaller, wondering what I'd gotten myself into, and wondering when I'd feel safe again.

"Later, on the county line, we stopped at an all-night gas station. Russ went in to buy cigarettes, leaving me in the car again. I peeked in the back seat, just once. Jewelry, a box of prescription bottles, a fat roll of cash rubber-banded together, and a road map. The sight of these things makes my hands sweat, but I touch nothing.

"When Russ comes back, he's grinning. 'You did good, Jo. Most girls would've screamed.' He lights up, takes a drag, and then leans across the seat to kiss me. His lips are rough and taste of salt. I was so in love, and we were on our way to get married. Yeah, I know, stupid, huh?"

"You were young … you didn't know."

"I've been telling myself that for years now. Yet, I think *I did know* it was wrong. I didn't care. I only wanted away from my father, and I loved this man who was showering me with attention."

She describes the days afterward, including their wedding night in a KOA cabin, eating cold beans from the can. With a wistful sigh, she continues:

"Russ fell asleep with his head in my lap. We stayed up, listening to the wind in the pines, and for a second, I let myself believe we'd outrun our demons, or whatever was chasing us."

By the next morning, Russ demanded they move on. The miles piled up, and apparently, so did the secrets. Although still excited about their adventure together, Joanne stopped asking questions. She explains to me how Russ would get in these moods. How she became invisible, with only a shadow attached to his, moving their way through the world.

One morning, days later, she described how they drove down this long road to a cabin a friend of his said they could use. She isn't even clear which state they were in at that point—she'd lost track. I feel her crying into the head cradle.

"Are you okay, Joanne?"

She sniffles, and I reached over to my shelf, grab a tissue, and hand it to her.

"Yeah, I'll be fine. The memories are a bit much."

"I'm here to listen, but please…"

"No, no. I'm okay." She wipes her nose, clears her throat, and then goes on.

"Everything changed after we went down that dirt road. By this time, I missed my family. Only I knew my daddy would kill me if I ever showed back up on his doorstep. I felt ashamed to look Willow in the eyes again—what she must think of me. So, I kept silent and cried, but only ever in the shadows of darkness and away from my husband. He wouldn't stand for that—he expected me to be grateful. I questioned myself for months—why wasn't I grateful? Of course, that became easier to answer after long periods of isolation, way out in the woods, where he told me no one would ever find us. Or maybe he meant no one would ever find *me*."

"That sounds scary. Were you terrified all alone out in the woods?"

"Yes, and no. Wasn't that what I wanted all along? Wasn't it my wish to escape my family, run away with this amazing man, and never be seen again? Well, I learned—be careful what you wish for."

I continue working on her calves, slowly kneading her tight muscles and captively listening to her story. She had confirmed his first name as Russ early on in the story, but no mention of their last name, Blankenship. It wasn't a common name like Smith. It couldn't be a coincidence. The deceased man I'd found near Show Low *had* to be her husband.

I wonder if she knew he'd been so close by? Had he followed her here to Arizona? Or had she followed him? My mind whirls with the possibilities, and I want to divulge what I know, but also realize I could be wrong and it needs to be handled delicately.

"You must have missed your sister something terrible. You'd said you were close as kids?"

Her head bobbed in a slight nod in the cradle. "I really missed her badly after I'd been gone about six months, and then especially as the years passed by. I remembered the way Willow used to braid my hair. Late nights, the two of us whispering secrets to each other in our bedroom. The sound of her singing, and for that matter, my mother's singing in the kitchen, too. I wanted to call, but never had the opportunity for years. Russ made sure of that. Then, I wondered if they had even noticed I was gone. Russ told me over and over that no one was looking for me, which meant they didn't love me."

Her story is heartbreaking. Her massage time ends, and she clams up again after she dressed and looked me in the eyes. Again, another client who spills so much as a tabletop confession, but appears almost embarrassed once they're off the table.

She hands me her credit card, and I use the card reader insert on my phone to process her transaction. This time I pay attention and see Joanne M. Pooley as the name on the card, which was not what I was expecting and catches me off guard. Why had she registered at the community center under Blankenship? I decide not to ask.

"Seriously, Joanne. You have a lot on your conscience—anytime you'd like to talk, I'm here to listen."

She takes her card back and tucks it into its place in her wallet, closes up her purse, and hurries along.

I watch as her vehicle pulls out onto the road and drives away. Then I pick up my phone and dial Willow. She's answers immediately.

"We're nearly there … sorry we were so late, but we

had the best time!"

I hear Apple and Annie cheer that statement in the background.

"Am I on speakerphone?" I ask.

I hear a tone and then, "Not anymore. What's up, Libby?"

"I wanted to let you know I ran into Joanne. She opened up a lot to me about the time she left your family and eloped. I'm guessing you didn't tell her anything after our earlier conversation?"

"No. She wasn't home, and then I left for the lake. But she still deserves to know. So, you didn't tell her?"

"No, I didn't. And, yes, I agree she needs to know." I hesitate. "Maybe when we tell her, let's leave out the part where I knew it was probably her husband? Otherwise, she's going to question why I didn't tell her myself this afternoon?"

"I guess none of us knows for sure it's him. I mean, the guy used many aliases over the years from what I understand." She paused. "What exactly are you asking, Libby?"

That's a good question. *What is it I want?* I want to find out who killed Russ Blankenship, to get the cops focused in the right direction. Yet, Officer Chesky seems to have already veered away from me. Regardless, did I think Joanne was responsible? Is that the reason for my hesitancy? I'm not sure what to think, but I want a little more time.

"You are right, Willow. We have no idea exactly who the dead man is. Therefore, let's not upset Joanne. Let's give the police a little longer, and I'm sure they'll contact her if she truly is the next of kin."

She doesn't agree or disagree, but only says she's uncomfortable keeping anything from her sister. Then, she hangs up after saying they're nearly at my house.

CHAPTER TWENTY-TWO

I watch as Willow's truck slowly enters the drive and then parks. The twins bolt from the vehicle, saying their goodbyes, and run past me into the house.

"Wanna join us for dinner?" I ask my friend.

She agrees, following Shadow and me inside. I offer her a drink and she chooses a cup of coffee. I pour myself a glass of water, then turn toward the kitchen table at the same time Apple nearly runs me over, hurrying out the back door with Shadow hot on her heels.

It's Willow who finally brings it up, as she sets her mug down on the table.

"So, we're not actually going to tell her?" she says. "That's the plan?"

"I don't know what the plan is," I say, not knowing

how to navigate these sisters.

Willow pushes her hands through her hair and then leaves them there, elbows out like bug antennae. "I know she's your friend now, but she's been my sister much longer. You must trust me. This news will hurt her, and I think she deserves a little warning."

"But what if it turns out to be false information?" I say, surprised at how whiny my voice sounds. "What if we're not ready?"

Willow shakes her head. "You don't *get ready* for something like this."

"Who even says it's him?" I ask. "Maybe the guy wasn't Joanne's—"

Willow stares at me, unimpressed. "What, you think it's a total coincidence? How many men go missing with the exact same name—"

"I know." I try to imagine myself in Joanne's shoes, but I can't. From the stories she's confessed to me—some kind of side hustle she once called 'not exactly legal'. Is her husband's disappearance or death possibly connected to this criminal lifestyle?

"Okay," I say, almost whispering. "So, if it is him, what does that even change? She's already convinced he's not coming back."

"She might be a suspect, for one thing," Willow shrugs. "Or she might be in danger if someone else did it. Or she might just want to know before the police or reporters show up at her doorstep. Er, *my* doorstep."

I think about that—about some uniformed cop knocking at the door—about the formal words, the empty eyes, the questions. About Willow and me already knowing, and pretending we didn't, and all the ways that could boomerang back.

We sit in silence while the world outside rearranges itself. Apple and Annie come barreling in from the yard, cheeks red and wet, the dog spattered with mud and a feather caught in her collar. Shadow shakes off in the doorway, decorating the tile with brown splatters.

The girls ignore them. They zero in on the pan of banana bread I left on the counter. Apple reaches for it, but Annie slaps her hand away, always the enforcer.

"We're starving," Apple announces, as if this is news.

"Wash your hands first," I say. "Let's get dinner started."

Shadow circles the kitchen island, a low whine in her throat, sure there should be food that's hit the ground already. Apple's job is to peel the carrots. Shadow loves that Apple has this job, because she sneaks little curls of carrot peeling onto the floor. Annie ignores her sister's antics, not looking up from the green beans she's stringing over a chipped Pyrex.

Willow's using a chef's knife that Greg sharpened with an oilstone last week, and slices up the carrots. With every cut the knife sounds just a little bit closer to cutting straight through the oak butcher block. At our end of the counter, we continue our conversation.

I look down the counter at the stack of carrots, then over at Willow. "And if it's not him?" keeping my voice low, aware of the girls' antennae for drama. "What do we do? Pretend we don't know?"

Apple snorts. "Know what?" She's moved on to slicing rounds, and the pieces are getting steadily thicker.

Annie piles the green beans in the colander, rinses her hands, and wipes them on her jeans. "It's none of our business, Apple."

Willow blinks at her, and I can't tell if she's impressed by Annie's logic or unsettled because they had heard our conversation.

Shadow's nose remains glued to the floor, two feet from the kitchen trash can, picking up every bit of carrot peel in a trail across the floor.

"She'll figure it out," Willows says, voice tight. "If we don't say something now, and it turns out we knew and never said a word—"

The stovetop holds pots of boiling and simmering liquids. Annie checks the couscous, peels back the lid, and flinches at a puff of steam. "Gross. Is it supposed to look like frog eggs?"

"It's perfectly normal," I say, coming around the island, leaning over the couscous, and inhaling. "Smells so good. Give it another minute." I tap my knuckles against Annie's back in a way that is both affectionate and practical—onward, soldier.

Shadow runs for the front door as we all hear clattering. I peer around the kitchen wall and see Greg trudging in and shedding layers of work clothing, grimacing as I see pine needles and debris falling to the freshly vacuumed flooring. He looks bigger than he is, but there's a weariness in how he slumps against the wall when he removes and kicks his work boots aside. "Good evening," he says, voice pitched halfway between a sigh and a bark.

"Wanna clean up and then join us? Dinner is almost ready. Willow's joined us too."

He shakes his head and heads to the bathroom.

Shadow follows me back into the kitchen, and within minutes, Greg drops onto the nearest barstool and props his face with both hands onto the countertop. It always astonishes me how quickly men shower.

"You look tired," Willow comments. "Good day at work?"

He grunts, and pops open the beer bottle I handed to him.

"Teddy showed up at the job site," he says after taking a swig. "In the woods, you know? Near the old rim road. He was pretty worked up."

"He say why?" I ask.

Greg shrugs. "He hasn't heard from Joanne since they hit it off the other night. Said he texted her. He, uh, really likes her." Greg's tone shifts, something uncertain about it. "But, uh, actually I really don't know what the issue is, probably his own insecurities? But he's convinced she's hiding something."

Annie frowns. "He should talk to her. Not to you."

Greg's mouth quirks. "Yeah, well. He says I remind him of his dad. So I guess I'm who he's coming to these days."

Willow turns from the stove, stirs the sauce, and leans against the countertop. "I mean, they just started this … whatever it is. Hasn't it only been days?"

I look down at the countertop, at the shallow groove the knife has left on the edge. "And what about her husband?" I say under my breath.

Greg nudges my elbow with his. "It is new, isn't it? Is it strange that he's worried about an unreturned text?"

I shrug. "It seems too soon. I mean, she was here for a massage, and maybe she's just been busy?" As soon as it was out, I realize Willow hadn't known about Joanne coming to my place for massage therapy. I quickly divert attention to the meal, and it appears she missed my gaffe.

Apple licks sauce off her spoon, already planning the

next round of kitchen duty. Annie pretends not to care, but she's watching, eyes narrowed, as if she's decided this is the sort of thing she'll use against her one day.

I call out, "Dinner in five." Everyone falls in line, delivering their dishes to the table: carrot couscous, chicken smothered in a mushroom sauce, and a medley of fresh roasted vegetables.

Greg gets up to feed Shadow—who receives her bowl with grateful, slobbering devotion—and then Greg takes his seat at the head of the table.

CHAPTER TWENTY-THREE

The Tuesday morning vibe of the community center appears to be energetic, yet I can tell there's a letdown from an event just over and all the work that comes next. Right now, all I need is Beth. Shadow and I make our way through the building. Apple and Annie run off to the kids' area.

Beth is exactly where I expect her—at her desk. Today she's got her hair in a loose knot, reading glasses threatening to slip from her nose as she presses a phone between shoulder and cheek, scans a clipboard, and hand-signals for me to take a seat. On the wall behind her, the clock ticks twelve minutes slow. On her desk, a box labeled "Lost & Found," which was quite sizeable after our eventful fundraising weekend. Beth manages a half-smile and the "give-me-one-more-minute" finger.

I hover, checking my phone: four unread messages, two voicemails (both from Willow), and a text from my mom wishing 'Aunt Libby' a fun last few days with my nieces. I set the phone to vibrate and grab a community flyer ("Free Financial Literacy! With Pizza!").

Beth wraps up her call, shifting from project coordinator to friend.

"Libby, hey. I'm only seventy-two percent here, but shoot." She's already checking off something on her clipboard.

I lean in, low voice. "You said you'd call if you heard more from the—" I catch myself before saying cops, but Beth knows what I mean.

She eyes the others passing by her office, then turns her focus on me. "The storage unit? They got the warrant yesterday. Show Low police, along with the Navajo County Sheriff's Department, are supposedly going over everything this morning."

She says 'supposedly' with the flattened tone of someone who's already placed a five-dollar bet that they won't.

"So, did they get the security footage?" I ask.

"Working on it. Apparently, the storage place only keeps thirty days' worth, so it's likely they'll have something. If it captures photos of the perpetrators, it'll break the case wide open—" She grimaces. "Could be nothing though."

"Crazy how long it's taking them, right?"

Beth shrugs, and for a second looks older than I remember, shoulders hunched forward, defeated. "For now. Cops will call if they have other questions, but I told them everything I know."

I drum my fingers on the desk. So much of me wants to fill Beth in on the latest I've learned about Joanne, but I know I shouldn't. It's important to keep this bit close to the vest for now.

Something occurs to me. "Has Joanne been in recently? Or is she done volunteering?"

Beth closes her eyes, just for a moment. "I don't think I've seen her since the ball. What was with her that night? Seemed like she was out of sorts. Willow and her sister seem to have a lot of contention between them, don't they?"

I want to deny it, but I don't know what to say. I agree with her assessment but tell her I don't know either very well to comment.

Beth picks up her clipboard again, checking off a box and scribbling an illegible note. "Libby, are you okay?"

"Yeah," I say, "I'm fine. I mean, I wish I could be more helpful in finding the sculpture. And of course, finding a dead body is unsettling, but no, I'm … I'm fine."

Beth looks at me with something like pity, or maybe just exhaustion. "People steal stuff all the time, Libby. Ask Greg about the guy who used to pocket all the ketchup packets from the community fridge. Why would anyone do that?"

I giggle, imagining that.

Beth shrugs again, and this time her shoulders go so high they nearly cover her ears. "You ever get the feeling that nobody's actually in control of anything? It's as if all the adults are constantly fixing issues, and even when things are destroyed, we still have to act normal the next day. Ah well, part of life. Hey, don't worry, though. We'll be okay—the fundraiser was a success thanks to the last-minute donors and the great turnout."

I agree with her and realize how much she's had to deal with lately. I ask, "Do you need help today?"

Beth laughs—short, like a cough. "Yes, but I'm not sure you're the help I need. You look like you haven't slept in a week."

"You're not wrong. This last week has been something else," I admit.

She gives me a long look. "Could you check in on the kids' room real quick? I'm sure Apple and Annie have it under control, and then I can take over from them in about twenty minutes?"

It's easy to say yes to this, easier than finding the answer to the other mysteries. I follow her down the corridor, past the wall of volunteer headshots (every smile slightly forced), and into the multipurpose room, where Apple and Annie are orchestrating a highly energetic game of musical chairs with five preschoolers and only four chairs. The twins have command of the room: Annie is shouting rules in a voice that bounces off the linoleum; Apple is making up new ones every few seconds.

Beth ducks out, and I'm left standing with the children, the noise, and the smell of peanut butter, apples, and juice boxes. For ten minutes, I am referee and therapist. One boy sobs uncontrollably when he loses his chair; a girl bites another girl on the arm, then runs away, screaming that she's a shark. I do what I can: comfort, admonish, give up on discipline entirely.

Apple takes pity on me. "You can go, Aunt Libby," she says. "We'll take it from here."

I slink out, then back toward the desk. A man in a cable-knit sweater is still there, eyes glazed, as if expecting the center to deliver divine guidance at any moment.

My phone vibrates. It's Willow, again.

Call me! She's written.

I step outside and call. She picks up on the first ring, breathless, like she's been holding the phone to her face all along.

"You okay?" I ask.

"Are you?"

"Define okay."

Willow sighs. "Did you find out anything?"

"Well, nothing related to Russ' death. But I'm at the community center, and Beth says the police have search warrants now for the storage facility security footage. That may not be related, however, I am relieved to hear that *something* is being done there."

There's a moment of static silence.

We talk in circles for a minute, nothing new, just the same facts orbiting closer and closer to the thing neither of us will say: that a man, who *could* be Joanne's missing husband, is dead.

When I hang up, the sun is slanting over the parking lot, slicing through the cloud cover. I glance back at the center's front, shuddering at the thought of returning to the screeching kids. Instead, I head to Beth's office, figuring that's close enough to hear if something goes horribly wrong. Otherwise, Apple and Annie have the kids under control.

I open my phone and type Paul Sanchez into the browser. The results are instant, a middle-aged man, several addresses listed, but last known in Phoenix, and has had a multitude of jobs over the years, including the most recent ones being a middle-school basketball coach, and a wedding photographer. His profile mentions nothing about coin collecting.

I sit for a long time, staring at the note in my hand. I've come up with a phone number and contemplate whether I really want to call. The number is local—a 928 area code.

I dial the number.

Four rings, then a voice, soft and oddly familiar: "Hello?"

"Hi," I say. "I'm calling about the donation you made to the Heber Community Center? My name's Libby."

A pause. Then, "Yes?"

The voice is older, careful, masculine but with a cautious high pitch to it.

"Can I ask why you donated the coins?" Feeling silly by the obtusely direct question, I resist explanation, waiting to see if he'll answer.

There's a long pause, as if he is deciding whether to hang up or confess something. Finally, "I was clearing out my property after a fire nearly destroyed it. They were from my late wife's deceased grandmother—but I don't think they were of much value. Anyway, I decided the fundraiser might be a good spot for them. Hopefully, they brought in some money?"

I realize then that I've probably made a mistake. This man doesn't strike me as the suspicious sort. Seemed more like a lonely older man. "I'm sorry for your loss."

"Oh, my wife died years ago," the man says, the edge gone from his voice. "But I still like to think she's helping, somehow, and she'd have agreed with giving the coins away. Anyway, was that all you needed?"

I think about asking about the fire, but suddenly I feel ridiculous for calling. What did it matter *why* he donated coins? But there was another thing that I wondered about—I'd like to meet the man in person. "Are you still in the area? Near Heber?" With quick thinking, I added in, "We'd like to give you a gift card to thank you for the recent donation."

"Well, no. Used to live up there—had a place over in Show Low for many years. Unfortunately, after the fire destroyed my place, and my insurance company dropped me, I could never rebuild it. Anyway, I've moved out of the state to be closer to my ill sister. So, no, I no longer visit Rim Country, but I thank you anyway."

I thank him, say goodbye, and end the call. The second it ended, I wondered *when* he had moved. It was only last week that I chased down the address on Mitchell Road. How was it I got that address if he hadn't given it to Beth? Oh well, too late, as we'd hung up.

I see Beth through a window. She's outside the center, talking to another woman with a clipboard, her hands moving in wide arcs, face flushed with energy. She's already back at it, stamping out the next fire.

I let myself watch her for a second. Then, I pull the Post-It apart into tiny squares, and drop them one by one into the trash bin. I'm already mentally composing the next questions that keep swirling around.

Once the twins' volunteer shift is over, we pop over to a sandwich shop and indulge in hot deli sandwiches, chips, and sodas. I listen to their tales from the morning babysitting, thankful again I don't have young ones. Will Greg and I decide to go that route? We've rarely talked about it, which reminded me we should. Our wedding is three months away, and after today I feel we need to talk sooner than later.

"Weren't we going to do some wedding stuff while we're in town?" Apple asks me, drawing me away from my inner thoughts.

"Uh, yeah …" I totally forgot that was something I'd mentioned to them. "I guess with the fundraiser activities, it slipped my mind."

Annie bursts out with excitement. "We can make floral arrangements!"

"Won't they wilt before October?" Apple asks.

"Well, yeah, but we can prepare silk arrangements, too. We can do those now."

Good point, I think as I polish off the last bites of my sandwich. That won't help me discover who stole the sculpture from the storage unit, or how Russ' murder connected to the fundraiser. But my nieces are only here a short time, and I want to spend quality time with them. If this is what they want to do, then this is what we'll do. I pull out my phone and Google it. Sure enough, there were Walmart stores both in Payson and Show Low. And both were about thirty to forty-five minutes away.

I look up from my phone. "Guess we know what we're doing with the afternoon then, don't we?"

We finish our lunch, drop Shadow off at home, and then head to Payson.

CHAPTER TWENTY-FOUR

The next morning, I bribe the twins with donut holes, and ignore their escalating tension over who gets to decide on which flowers to use for the decorative arch they talked me into buying.

Apple grins. Annie, already dusted with powdered sugar, does a double-thumbs-up. "We're ready to decorate the arch and we're not afraid of getting our hands dirty."

I take one look at her sugar encrusted fingers and hand them both napkins. "Let's finish eating first, then you're free to work."

I got them started by cutting some of the silk flower stems and wire-tying them to the arch now set up in the living room. I turn to Apple for approval, only to see her hands on her hips.

"We want to surprise you, though, Aunt Libby."

Annie's frown turns to a smile. "We have some really good ideas. Trust us."

"Okay, Okay. I'll leave you guys to it." I say, walking away, only slightly nervous about how it'll turn out.

When I walk back into the kitchen, I see my laptop and notepad sitting at the end of the breakfast bar. Something catches my eye—a yellow envelope labeled "DONATION: COINS." I forgot I had picked this up from Beth's office. I flip open the flap and see a folded letter, half a business card, and a single-page printout with "Sanchez, P." at the top. The address is the one I had gone to. But we already knew that's not where he lived, so where was it that he had lived? The place that burned down.

I open my laptop, search for the Sanchez address: nothing useful. I tack on Show Low, and get a few property listings, none of which fit. Next, I try 'Show Low home destroyed in fire'. There are several, and I have no idea which belonged to the Sanchez family.

What ties did Paul Sanchez have to Martin Spiegel and the Mitchell Road Mobile Home Park? I open a new search window. "Show Low + coin collectors" brings up a single newspaper clipping. "Show Low Man Arrested in Multi-State Coin Fraud." The name I find, in the third paragraph, is "Russ Blankenship."

What?

In a kind of trance, I click through multiple articles that lead in various directions. There's only the one mention of Russ Blankenship's arrest. From this, there's no way for me to determine if they are the same coins that were donated to the center. Coincidence?

My phone rings. Beth.

"Hey, Beth, what's up?"

"Listen, Officer Chesky called and says he has something to show us."

"Oh?"

"He can come by the center. How soon can you get here?"

Five minutes, I tell her, and already have my shoes on by the time she says goodbye.

"Girls, I have to run to the community center for a little bit. Wanna go with or are you good here on your own until I return?"

"No, we need to finish. We're fine until you get back."

"I'm leaving Shadow with you."

"Okay!" they reply in unison.

* * *

When I walk through the front doors, I see Beth sitting at her desk and Officer Chesky in the seat across from her. I take the one next to him after we greet each other. He immediately gets down to business.

Beth plugs in a cable from his laptop to her monitor and gets it turned around for us to see.

"You're going to want to see this footage," he says as he opens his laptop, pushes a few buttons, and the screen comes to life.

We see the driveway to get to the storage unit. My heart beats faster when I see my 4Runner round the corner.

"You can't think…"

Chesky holds up a hand. "Hold on, Libby. Just watch."

We watch as Willow and I file out of the vehicle. Shortly afterward, a car pulls up behind us—the teens that

Beth sent over to help us. In the footage, we see two of the football players at the back of the 4Runner, sizing up the load they're about to lift. While they do that, I open the lock on the storage door and roll it open.

Chesky stops the footage. "See right there."

"Uh, no. Musta missed it," I mumble, and Beth shakes her head, too.

He presses the button on his laptop to go back several seconds. Then he slows down the replay. "Right there." He points to the ground next to the roll-up door.

I nod, not remembering how I'd tossed the keyring and the lock onto the ground.

"Now look," he points out.

He slows the replay even further. Arms loaded, the teenage boys inch their way toward the unit and disappear inside. Willow and I follow them. As soon as we are out of sight, a shadowy figure moves into the frame.

"Right there!" Chesky stops the footage. The shadowy figure vanishes. *And so did the keys!*

Beth pops up to the edge of her seat. "Wait, can we see that again?"

"Sure." He replays it, and this time slows it to the slowest possible replay.

Beth gets excited. "Libby, this clears you! Someone stole the keys while all of you were inside the unit."

Her words hit me strangely, as I knew all along I hadn't 'lost' them.

"If someone stole the storage keys, how is it possible I had a set of keys the next time we returned to the unit? How did the set of keys, minus the one key, find its way back into my purse?"

We watch and rewatch the footage at different playback

speeds, and none of us can figure it out.

Beth scratches her head. "Are there any other camera angles we haven't seen?"

"We are still waiting for the storage facility to send us footage from the cameras coming in and out of the facility, but we felt this was the most important one since it shows movements in and out of that exact unit."

"And there isn't anything else that shows a clearer picture of that person in all black?" I ask.

"Unfortunately, there isn't."

As happy as I am to see this development, it certainly doesn't answer all the questions. Beth notices me deflate after Chesky leaves.

"It's okay, Libby. We'll find out who stole that sculpture. Don't worry."

CHAPTER TWENTY-FIVE

By the time I make it home, Shadow tells us she needs to go outside, and Apple volunteers to take her, while I put a kettle on. Annie has hung a sheet up across the living room entrance so I can't see their handiwork. She guards it while Apple runs the dog outside.

"When Uncle Greg gets home," she informs me. "And not before."

I check my phone and see that there is a text message from Greg. He suggests we take the girls to The Mill for dinner. I shoot him a thumbs up and then pour myself a cup of tea. Once the girls trust that I won't peek behind the curtain, they raid the fridge for snacks and then run off to their room together.

Going back to my laptop, I search for more information

on Paul Sanchez or Martin Spiegel. Even though the police may clear me in the storage unit theft, I can't help but worry about getting caught up in the murder mystery. There's still a killer on the loose, and it certainly is not me.

How did Sanchez and Spiegel connect to the murder of Russ Blankenship? *Maybe they didn't?* A lightbulb came on. I had completely forgotten about Patty and the painting from the silent auction. I pick up my phone and call Beth.

When she picks up, it's obvious she has her hands full at the community center. *Does the woman ever stop?* Quickly, I ask about delivering the painting. She explains that the funds still haven't been received. They've reached out several times, but Beth isn't confident the lady will come through. She covers the phone, shouting something.

"Listen, I've gotta go, Libby."

The line goes dead. I stare at the half-completed chore list on the fridge, but feel the familiar coil of anxiety tighten around my ribs.

When Greg gets home, he kicks off his shoes and flops onto the armchair. "You look like you've had a day," he comments.

"I talked to the police earlier," I say, relating everything I learned there.

Greg shrugs. "Well, that's good! We know you had nothing to do with that theft, and now, so do they. You should be thrilled."

"I am."

"But?"

"I also talked to Paul Sanchez."

"Who's that?"

"The one who donated the coins. I probably forgot to

tell you that the coins actually got delivered to the center—I figured that out when I found them in Beth's office."

"Oh?"

"But fast forward—I've talked to the guy and I really think it's a dead end. He was nice enough—a widower clearing out belongings after a house fire and hoping the coins would help in the fundraiser."

"Oh, jeez."

"Yeah. I think that line of questioning is dead, and so I'm baffled." Then I remembered I hadn't filled him in on the rest. "OH! But massive revelation—Joanne's ex—er, missing husband, is Russ Blankenship."

Greg gives one shoulder a shrug. "Okaaay. And? I don't recognize that name…"

"That's the same name as the ID found on the dead guy in that mobile home!"

"Oh, no. Are you serious? It was Joanne's husband?"

"Well, I can't be sure. Still waiting on the coroner's office." I take a deep breath.

"Okay, so once they officially know the identity of the man, surely the police will notify her."

I lower my eyes, embarrassed. "It just seems I should give her a heads up."

He lets out a long whistle. "No wonder you've looked tired lately. That's a lot to hold onto, Libs. But, you know the police still have work to do. There's nothing to tell her yet."

I poke my head into the girl's room and let them know to get cleaned up for dinner out at The Mill.

Annie jumps off the bed excitedly. "Uncle Greg's home? He hasn't gone into the living room yet, has he?"

I shake my head and feel the air rush when both girls

push by me, running down the hallway.

"Uncle Greg!" They flank him, taking his hands and asking him to close his eyes. "Aunt Libby, you too, close your eyes." Apple grabs my hand and they lead both of us into the living room.

After some whispering, the girls shout, "Open your eyes!"

I open my eyes to see an exquisite array of flowers arranged beautifully on the arch. Surprised, I see they'd strung fairy lights through the clusters of flowers, the length of the arch, illuminating it perfectly.

"Oh, my goodness, girls! This is so beautiful. You did all this today?"

Greg adds, "Oh wow. You guys didn't buy it this way in Payson yesterday?"

I shook my head. "No, they wanted to decorate it and surprise us."

"That's amazing!"

"You two are hired to help decorate the rest of the place when the time comes."

Apple and Annie, very pleased with themselves, high-five each other.

Shadow looks resentful as I throw a cookie in her kennel and tell her we'll be right back. On the drive over, Annie questions whether they serve macaroni and cheese. We laugh since that's what she's asked to eat at nearly every meal. She asks, "Do you think there are people who only eat cheese, and nothing else?"

I turn in my seat. "Yes. They're called 'dead.'"

Greg laughs. Apple rolls her eyes, but dinner out, including a huge helping of macaroni and cheese for Annie, turns out to be just what we all needed. As I watch my loved ones converse, I can't believe we are only two days away from my nieces going home. How had the time gone so fast?

In so many ways it's gone fast, but what's crawling at a snail's pace is information from the police. And why is my summer consumed by more bad guys, more crime? Regardless, I know that if I didn't do more to figure it out, I would not settle into wedding planning.

That's it. Tomorrow, I'm going to drive over to Show Low. I keep feeling I should divulge my knowledge of Joanne being married to Russ Blankenship. Hopefully, I can talk to Officer Chesky. Also, maybe a visit to Patty, at the mobile home park, will reveal *something*.

"Girls, are you volunteering tomorrow?"

Apple perks up. "Ms. Coggins says there is a youth art class tomorrow, and the teacher needs assistants. I'd *love* to do that!"

Annie nods her head vigorously as she chews.

"Okay—what time?" I ask.

They look at each other questioningly.

"It's okay. I'll text Beth to ask."

The two look relieved and then chatter away about how fun the community center is as I text Beth to work out the details.

Once we are at home, I serve up leftover apple pie and ice cream. Then we settle in for a show on Netflix, and I watch everyone's eyes get heavy. Soon enough, I tuck the girls into their beds, step out into the hallway, and sigh. On the couch, Greg softly snores, exhausted from a long day of physical labor and a belly full of barbecue ribs.

The house is quiet except for the slow tick of the kitchen clock and the distant sound of Beth's voice, echoing in my head:

"You ever get the feeling that nobody's actually in control of anything?"

Yes. All the time.

But for once, I want to pretend otherwise.

The drive to Show Low has become a familiar one, I realize as I drop off the girls at the community center and then pull out onto Highway 260 and head east. Looks like a wide-open road this morning, which isn't always necessarily the case. I turn up the volume, listening to an old favorite, *Hold On,* by Wilson Philips. I belt out the repeating chorus as though I'm on stage with the band. Smiling, I remember how long I've loved the song and how empowered it makes me feel.

As radio ads dominate the next few minutes, I notice a truck in my rearview mirror coming up on me at tremendous speed. My pulse surges as I try to decide the best thing to do—slow down, he may hit me; speed up and everything becomes more dangerous with the curves in the road that I know are up ahead. Before the thoughts make it through my brain, the truck with a male driver passes me on a double-yellow. As he does, I see a female passenger with a hat and sunglasses on, barely able to see over the dashboard.

They quickly disappear down the road, and I settle back into my drive, hoping they make it safely wherever they are going. Better yet, hopefully there's a cop ahead and the driver will get a hefty ticket before he kills someone.

Unfortunately, there aren't any cops along the route, until I come upon traffic backed up for miles outside the Show Low city limits. Crawling toward the intersection of US60, I see where they are diverting traffic. I notice a flash of mangled black metal, but not much more than that as the officers reroute traffic down the nearest streets.

By the time I pull up at the police station over an hour later, I feel frazzled and nearly forget my purpose for being here. My phone chimes, pulling me back into the moment.

"Hey, Willow. What's up?"

"Libby, where are you? I need to get to Show Low!"

"Whoa, you sound scared. What's going on?"

"It's Joanne. She called and is on the way to the hospital—something about an accident."

My breath catches. "Willow, I just got to Show Low. What do you need me to do?"

"Oh no. I was hoping you could drive me there. I'm a mess, Libby, and shouldn't drive."

"Okay, slow down. I'll go to the hospital and report back. Will that help? I can also see if Greg or someone else can drive you here. But let's see what the situation is first. If she called you, that's a good sign, right?"

There was a brief pause. "Yeah. I suppose so, but she didn't sound good. Okay, call me as soon as you see her and know anything."

I agree, ditching plans to talk to Officer Chesky, and peel out of the police station. Before pulling out into traffic, I Google the address and follow the directions. My heart races, wondering about that stupid, reckless guy driving the black truck. *Had he T-boned her at that intersection? Was that even the accident she was involved in? Wait—what was she doing in Show Low?*

Pulling into the visitor parking, I tell myself to relax. I turn off the engine and hurry inside the emergency room, asking for Joanne. They have me sit in the waiting room and say they'll be with me in a minute.

CHAPTER TWENTY-SIX

Walking into the ER, I hear all the monitors beeping; I pull back the curtain and see Joanne, her face pale, horribly bruised, and dried blood matting her hair. The machines, synchronized with the rising and falling of the patient's chest, bring so many memories of horrible hospital visits flooding back. My father's death when I was a teenager is the worst memory I have. But since then, it seems I keep finding myself in hospitals—and this needs to stop.

A nurse checks a drip line and comments that they are prepping Joanne for surgery before skirting by me and disappearing again. Passively, I hear something about head trauma. I take Joanne's small hand, praying she makes it through, and thinking of Willow and how she only recently got her sister back. She can't lose her now.

No sooner does the thought cross my mind, I look up and Willow is standing there with her hand over her mouth. Tears crash over her bottom eyelids and spill onto her cheeks. I walk over and envelop her in my arms.

"She's going to be okay." It's all I can really say as we have to believe it to be true.

"Wh—what happened? She called me. She, she was … was talking." Willow's eyes take in the machinery all around us.

"I'm sure the nurse will return any moment to fill you in. They said there's been head trauma—and I know she's heavily medicated."

Willow collapses onto a nearby chair. "But…"

"I know." I stand over her with my hand on her shoulder. "Let's see what they say; we need to stay strong for her."

We sit silently in prayer until another nurse appears. She explains how the scans show bleeding on the brain. Nothing catastrophic, but they have to release that pressure. The doctor is on his way, and they will take her into surgery.

Willow sobs through her questions, and the nurse gently assures her they will take care of Joanne. After sitting with us a few more minutes, she guides us to the waiting room and also points out the chapel to Willow.

"You might be more comfortable there." The nurse turns away, promising we'll hear from the doctor as soon as the surgery in done.

Soon after, the friends who drove Willow to Show Low surround her, offering their thoughts and prayers, and they guide us down the hallway to the chapel. I gently touch her shoulder before she walks inside. "Willow, I will be back."

I give her another hug and then leave them in the chapel.

$* * *$

My mind weighs heavily on everything that's happened. On Joanne, the man who died, and wondering why all these things were happening. Two sisters who have recently found each other, yet life being so fragile, it might separate them again. Tragic. I can't seem to get rid of the memory of the speeding black truck, flashing dangerously by me. *Was* that *the accident she was in?*

Knowing I won't get those answers yet, I push them away for now and concentrate on driving safely to the mobile home park. Of course, I'll need to get back to the police station, but first, I want to talk to Patty at the mobile home park. There is something strange about her silent auction bid for a painting she can't afford—or is that an unfair presumption on my part? Maybe I can help Beth either get the money, or at least officially cross Patty off the list so she can notify the next bidder.

As I pass through the entrance, the community is as quiet as it was the last time I drove in. I keep my eyes open for the old dog, but I don't see Tiger anywhere. I park next to the curb a couple of doors down from Mr. Spiegel's home, glancing around, but not noticing anyone peering through their windows.

It's remarkable what a quiet, almost deserted, place this is. I close my car door gently so as not to disturb the peace. I step softly, almost tip-toeing, up the walkway to Patty's front door. Then I chuckle to myself, wondering why I'm behaving this way.

After several knocks, it's evident no one is home. Either

that, or she's fantastic at pretending not to be. I lean in close to the door, listening for any sign of life inside after my last round of pounding. Still nothing, so I slip away and get back into my vehicle.

Why would she bid on that painting and then disappear? She hasn't returned any of Beth's phone calls. Oh well, my advice to Beth will be to call the next person on the bidding list because we've given this one plenty of opportunity to claim her item.

Now, back to the police station, another stop at the hospital, then home.

CHAPTER TWENTY-SEVEN

Officer Chesky wasn't in, and no one else was helpful. I wondered whether part of that might be them still suspecting I'm involved. No matter what, they simply disregarded my snooping around. Fine. *Why did it matter if I found out who killed Russ Blankenship, anyway?*

After striking out at the police station, it was clear I needed to get back to my family and leave this whole murder business behind.

A little niggle in my gut signaled that the answer to the question is Beth and the fundraiser. Also, Willow and Joanne. Even though I'd only befriended all of them this summer, I'd found myself entwined in their lives somehow. And friends help friends, right?

It's nearly three in the afternoon when I'm back in the

hospital parking lot. Checking my phone, I'd missed a call from Greg. I punched the button to return the call.

"Hey, there…" he answered. "When will you be home?"

"Unfortunately, not for a little while. I'm at the hospital."

"What? In Show Low?"

"Yes. Joanne was in a horrible accident—it's a long story."

"Oh no. Will she be okay?"

"I'm about to find out; I'm not sure."

"What was she doing in Show Low?"

That was a good question. "I really don't know. But listen, she went into surgery several hours ago, and I hope we have an update by now. Let me go get more information, and then I'll call you back when I'm on my way home. Sound good?"

"You be really careful."

"Promise. Hey, how are you and the girls doing?"

"Great! After the girls' volunteer work, we went on a fantastic hike and got a little fishing in as well. Shadow was in heaven with all the activities. The girls seemed to enjoy fishing, but I don't think Apple was too excited when I told them they had to gut and clean their own fish. Annie did great—got right into it."

I laugh, picturing exactly what their expressions would have been. "So, we're having fish for dinner?"

"If you'd like. Or, we can freeze?"

"Sounds good to me. You three surprise me."

"Will do. Love you!"

I hang up and walk into the waiting room to find Willow and her friends chatting a bit more cheerfully than when I'd left them earlier.

"Any updates?" I ask Willow.

"The surgeon just came in and said everything went well. She's in recovery right now, but we should be able to see her within the next hour or so. However, she will still be sedated. They don't expect to wean her from the meds until tomorrow at the earliest."

"I'm happy it sounds positive. Anything I can do for you?"

"No, no. But thank you, Libby. I appreciate your being here for her before I could be. We're getting a motel nearby, so I'll have support until Joanne is ready to go home."

"Fantastic. Then I'm going to head out, but please call me with any updates." I turn before remembering something. "Hey, do you know what she was doing here in Show Low?"

Willow's brunette friend piped up. "No one does. In fact, her car is still at Willow's—no one knew she'd left town."

Another vision of that black truck dangerously whizzing past me gives me a chill. I shake it off. "Well, I guess we'll learn those details when she wakes up."

"If she remembers," Willow sadly adds. "We're not sure how much of her memory she'll retain."

I nod, then reach out to give Willow one last hug before I leave. Walking out to the parking lot, I give Greg a call back, letting him know I'll be home within the hour.

I get fifteen minutes down the road before my phone rings again. It's Officer Chesky. I punch the button on my steering wheel to answer the call hands-free. He needs to see me right away, and I tell him I can be there within twenty minutes. Then I call Greg back and apologize for missing dinner after all.

* * *

When I arrive at the substation, I'm led to his office by the front desk clerk, and surprised to see Beth sitting there.

Officer Chesky greets me, and Beth adds, "He thinks there's a big lead on the sculpture theft."

"That's great. After the day I've had, I'd love some good news."

Beth's voice turns to concern. "What happened?"

"Joanne was in a horrible accident—here, in Show Low."

"Oh, no! Willow?"

"She wasn't with her—not involved in the accident. She's there now though, at the hospital."

"Ladies, you're going to want to see this…" Chesky interrupts, as he opens his laptop and turns on the TV screen to share the images.

Both Beth and I twist around to see the screen. We see the timeline at the bottom, noting it's the date of the storage unit break-in and he's already skipped ahead to just after midnight.

This is a different view from what we've seen already. The storage unit lot is dark, but the security lights are on. A van—not the community center's, but a rented U-Haul—pulls up. Two figures get out, one tall and wide, the other much slighter, hair up in a messy bun. The tall one moves with a weird familiarity, like an ex-jock gone to seed. They use a key to open the main gate.

"Do you recognize either person?" Chesky asks.

I inhale, then let it out slowly. "I can't be certain, but could the tall one be Russ Blankenship?"

Chesky's face goes slack. "What? How…?"

I nod. "I don't know. It's hard to see in this footage versus what I saw splayed out on the floor."

"What about the other one in the frame?"

I study the footage and feel sick. "That's Joanne, his wife." I say, surprised at how flat my own voice sounds. "Her hair … and those shoes. I'm sure it's her."

Beth gasps.

Chesky watches us, pen poised over his legal pad. "How do you know this? I thought you didn't know him?"

"Um, I know Joanne. Her sister, Willow, as well. I learned only recently that Joanne has a husband named Russ Blankenship. It's why I came by earlier to see you—to give you that latest tidbit."

He gives a gruff harrumph. "Well, they're in and out in less than fifteen minutes. The guy takes three crates, with the woman carrying a duffel and something wrapped in a mover's blanket. Any idea what was in those?"

Beth has a horrified expression. She looks at me, and I know what she's thinking: the fundraisers, the donations, the weirdly expensive sculpture—and how could Joanne be involved?

"It's probably the Pat Schellinger piece," I say. "Our most valuable donation that could have benefitted our community for years to come."

Chesky nods. "We're working on tracking the van rental. We'll see if that matches up with your identification of the driver."

Beth makes a noise, halfway between a sigh and a groan. "She knew. She knew the whole time, and just—"

I expect her to get angry, to swear or pound the table, but she deflates. "I don't get it. *Why?*"

"Willow indicated to me that her sister has a past, but

she didn't divulge a whole lot. Joanne also shared a little with me, but I thought the criminal behavior came from her missing husband. I would never have suspected she was involved."

Chesky clicks stop on the video and closes the laptop. "Missing husband?"

"When she arrived in Heber this summer, that's how she put it to me—that he was missing. In further conversation, it sounds more like he left her. But who really knows?"

Beth's mouth twists, as if she's about to say something sharp, but she bites it down.

Chesky turns to me. "Is this the same Joanne who is in the hospital? You mentioned when…"

"Yes." I nod, but my mind spins off in new directions. Joanne. Russ. All the stolen goods. But also, Willow—*how much did she know?*

Chesky stands. "That's all for now. If you think of anything else, call me. We know where to find Joanne, so that's my next step. Don't alert her sister—stay out of it and let us do our job. Okay, Libby?"

I'm wounded—*why do I always get a lecture about that?*

We leave the station in silence. Outside, stars have taken over the night sky. Beth walks to her car, then turns back. "What are we supposed to do now?"

I don't have an answer, so I say, "We could eat pancakes. That fixes things for like ten minutes."

Beth laughs—the kind that cracks the tension for a moment. "You're buying."

We hit a local diner. It's nearly empty except for a trucker in camo and a couple of teenage boys sharing fries and a milkshake. Beth orders a short stack and black coffee; I get a veggie omelet, hoping Beth will share some of her pancakes.

We sit in silence for a while. The server drops off our plates, also without a word.

Finally, Beth says, "I keep thinking about the last time I saw Joanne. There's something deeply wrong in her life."

I nod. What more could I say given what we've learned at the police station?

Beth chews her pancake and frowns. "You ever think about how, if you're raised with secrets, lying just comes naturally? Like, it's easier than telling the truth because you don't even see that line anymore."

I stir my coffee. "I guess this type of thing goes on in many families—all walks of life."

She looks at me. "Does Willow know she was involved in the theft?"

I shake my head. "I hope not. At least, I don't think she knows about this theft, and I'd like to tell her this latest bit before the cops do."

Beth pokes at the last bit of her pancake. "Chesky warned you. But I know what you mean. Willow is a good person. I certainly don't want to lose her. She's been good for the community center, but…"

"Hey, none of that," I say, and we both laugh at how ridiculous and obvious it sounds. "If we are all judged by the things our siblings do, what kind of crazy world would that be?"

When we part ways, Beth hugs me so tight my bones click. "Let me know if you need help talking to those sisters. Don't do anything stupid, Chesky will be all over you," she says.

"Define stupid," I say, and then she just rolls her eyes.

I drive home, windows down, the mountain air cool and refreshing.

CHAPTER TWENTY-EIGHT

Knowing I only had two more days with my nieces, the very last thing I wanted to do was to leave them again. But Joanne lying in a hospital weighed on me, too. And sitting at the bottom of my gut was the stress of telling Willow the new information I had.

Apple's phone rang, and I watched as she got super excited. "Hold on. Let me ask." She turned to me. "Aunt Libby, Ms. Coggins needs help at the community center. Would it be okay if we went over there this morning? We'd be back after lunch…"

Annie perked up from staring at her plate. *"Pleaassse!"*

"If that's what you'd like to do today, it's fine with me." I'd barely got the words out and Apple was already confirming with Beth that they could work this morning.

When she hung up, the twins hurriedly finished the rest of their breakfast. As they ran down the hallway to their room to get ready, Apple shouted, "Beth said she'd pick us up in half an hour!"

I love their enthusiasm. My smile still hadn't faded when Greg rounded the corner into the kitchen.

"What's that all about?" he asked, turning his head as they blew past him.

"The girls are excited to work at the community center again. I guess they're meeting a bunch of new friends and really enjoying it."

"Wow, if we have kids one day, I sure hope they have this same work ethic."

"Me too!"

* * *

When I walk into the hospital, I see no sign of the police anywhere. I find Willow's friends sitting in the waiting room.

"How's Joanne? Where's Willow?"

They take turns filling me in on the latest, starting with telling me that Willow is with Joanne. Two visitors at a time, and one of them had just returned to the waiting room. Joanne is awake this morning, but so far still quite groggy and doesn't appear to remember anything. They attempt to reassure me that all of it's normal and then give me her room number so I could go join Willow.

When I step into the elevator, there's a man already in there. I don't recognize him, but there was something about him that made me feel I should. My pulse increases. I take in his features: average height and weight, dark cropped hair, bushy eyebrows, and dark eyes. He wore a nice gray collared short-sleeved shirt and black leisure slacks. I try to keep my eyes on the elevator floor, but can't help taking awkward peeks. *Where did I know this man from?*

He steps off at the floor before Joanne's. False alarm, wasn't anyone I knew. Then that earlier dreadful feeling came over me; I have to inform Willow about her sister, who was seen stealing from the storage unit. I can't even think of how to approach Joanne with the conversation and suspect that will have to wait. And maybe it's best I don't—the police should break it to her.

Still wrestling with what I would do, I walk into her room—many machines are blinking and beeping. Willow looks up and immediately crosses the room to greet me.

"She woke up!"

"I heard—that's fantastic."

"She tires easily, and she just fell asleep again."

"Um, Willow, can we go somewhere private to talk for a moment? While she's sleeping?"

She looks at Joanne hesitantly, but ultimately agrees. "For a few minutes. She could wake up again at any time."

We stroll down the hall and find a private little corner with a couple of chairs. I sit across from Willow and tell her everything Beth and I had seen on the video.

She listens without interruption, doesn't even blink at the parts about Joanne or Russ or the stolen sculpture. When I finish, she says, "Well, shit. That's a lot."

I nod. "Yeah. I thought you'd freak out more."

Willow shrugs. "Okay, yeah. Maybe I'm surprised I'm not reacting more, too. Honestly, nothing surprises me anymore."

I want to ask if she's mad, or scared, or disappointed, but the dialogue hangs in the air between us.

Instead, I say, "At least she survived the accident. I'm not sure what comes next, but I felt you should know."

"I guess that's it for my volunteering with Beth." Willow hangs her head sadly.

"Oh, I don't know about that." I take her hand. "You weren't involved."

Her eyes dart around and then find mine again. "I didn't know a thing—I promise you, Libby."

"I know that."

"So, I guess the police will come?"

I nod. "I'm actually surprised they aren't here already, and I really wanted to tell you myself before they showed up. But, uh, can you act surprised when they tell you? I wasn't supposed to say anything."

She agrees. "Thank you for telling me, Libby."

We watch several people pass by in the hallway. Then I ask, "You ever wish she'd left him—er, Russ—and had started over elsewhere?"

"Every single day. I actually thought she had. When she called me asking for help, I thought that was the moment. She'd left, and she would get her life back on track. Now I feel foolish."

We're quiet for a long time. Then, softly, she says, "Thanks for telling me first, though."

"Of course," I say, and mean it. "Has Joanne said anything about the accident?"

"No, nothing."

"There's another little piece I feel you should know." I hesitate but then launch in with what I'd seen with the high school football player and how I suspected they knew each other better than only volunteering at the community center.

That was a surprise to Willow. And neither of us knew the details yet about Joanne's accident.

When we make it back to Joanne's room, her eyes are still closed, and she looks so peaceful. I beg out, saying I need to get back to the girls. Willow tells me she'd be in contact later, when she's learned more.

As the elevator bumped to a halt on the ground floor, and the doors opened, the man in the gray shirt was waiting for me.

CHAPTER TWENTY-NINE

Trying not to make eye contact with the man again, I scoot to his left to get around him.

"Miss?" he says calmly, reaching out, touching my arm.

I recoil, glancing around, looking for witnesses. "Me?"

He nods. "Miss, I've seen you around and wonder if I could ask you a few questions?"

I walk away from the elevator bank, toward the lobby, where I see more people loitering around. "Who are you?"

"Martin Spiegel."

I slow down near the front check-in desk, but at a complete loss for words.

"Pardon me, but I've seen you in town—at the police station; we passed in the hallway, but I'm not sure if you noticed. And again, here at the hospital. I was upstairs."

His finger points toward the ceiling. "Um, can we start with … er, what's your name?"

Posturing myself, knowing that someone died in this man's home, I decide to take control of the conversation. "No. First, what are *you* doing here? Let's start there."

"Sure. Sure." He points to a cluster of empty chairs at the far side of the room. "Let's take a seat."

I walk toward the chairs and plop down on the one closest to the sliding glass doors.

He clears his throat. "Listen, I'm dealing with some strange events lately. Some of this is going to sound crazy if you aren't who I think you might be. So, bear with me."

My eyebrows lift. "Who do you think I am?"

"I think you're the woman who found a dead body in my home."

I nod. "That's true."

He laces his fingers together. "I believe the police are looking at both of us as 'persons of interest' in the case."

Another brief nod from me.

"I had nothing to do with it, and I don't know the man they found in my home. I suspect the same is true for you?"

This piques my interest as I was under the impression that he *did have* a relationship with Russ Blankenship. I choose to wait before hitting him with my questions, wanting him to reveal what he knows first.

He proceeds. "Listen, there's so much to the story, but there's a history that I've reminded the officers about. I have evidence. They seem to have disregarded me, the past police reports I've filed, and the evidence I have. I believe it's directly related to what's happened recently."

"What is your relationship to Russ Blankenship?" I ask him directly.

His brows knit together. "What?"

I wait.

"I don't understand..." he runs his hand through his thick black hair. "How do *you* know Russ?"

"I don't."

"What does he have to do with this conversation?"

"Because he was murdered in your home..."

Martin abruptly stands. "That's not true. Where'd you hear that?" His shouting attracts attention.

"The police."

He turns around and retakes his seat. "Oh. Okay. I know what you're referring to—the ID that was found, right? Well, I have long since confirmed that the dead man was definitely not Russ. I couldn't say who he was, never seen him before in my life."

"Then why are the police still hanging on to that theory?"

"I don't know, but I think maybe you just haven't received the newest information. The DNA results came back today and prove I'm correct—it was not Russ."

Relieved to learn it's not Joanne's husband, I find myself confused all over again about the connections. "Who was the man stabbed inside your home then?"

"I have no idea."

"What was your connection to Russ—you clearly know who he is?"

He explains how they'd met in their youth, had gone their separate ways after several run-ins with the law—all under the age of eighteen. Years later, Russ contacted him asking for a place to stay while he got back on his feet—for him and his wife. This tracks with information I'd already learned, leading me to believe Marty isn't feeding me a line of crap now.

"Earlier you said you had 'evidence.' What's that about?"

"I think I know who did it. I'm sure he was after me—so that would explain why it happened in my home. But unfortunately, that means it's a case of mistaken identity."

"Okay, I'm listening."

"The man's name is Paul Sanchez, and we have a long history together. He has tried to ruin my reputation since a fire destroyed his house and my insurance company found it to be arson."

My stomach lurches. *There was a connection.*

Martin carefully laid out the entire scene years prior: how he showed up at the Sanchez residence for the inspection, joined by the fire chief, and they methodically went through all the evidence. Martin Spiegel wrote up his insurance report and thought that would be the end of it. How wrong he was.

"For years afterward, this man has stalked me. I've filed complaints and restraining orders against Paul Sanchez. Even so, and as recently as a few months ago, I've received threatening letters from him."

"And you've brought this to the department's attention?"

"You bet I have!" His face splotched red, and he clenched his fists. "I can show you."

I looked around the hospital lobby, watching people coming and going in various moods. "Yes, I'd like to see what you have. And by the way, my name is Libby Madsen."

"And why were you at my house that day? How did you become involved in this?"

I explained everything from the beginning as we left

the building and walked through the parking lot.

"I'll follow you—I know where we're going," I say, getting into my 4Runner.

* * *

I flip through the documentation that Martin Spiegel hands me. It tells an incredible story— about Paul Sanchez, as well as Russ Blankenship. Surprised, I set aside an eviction notice to remind myself to ask more questions.

There were pages and pages of text messages printed out that detailed specific threats. Some messages included photographs of job sites where Marty worked. It was chilling to see actual evidence of his stalker.

"Why did the police disregard this?"

"Nowhere in here does it name him. See this phone number?—burner phone. He switches them out regularly. Look here," he points to several pages laid out in date order. "Different numbers on each of these."

"And they haven't been able to match phone numbers to him?"

He shakes his head, looking defeated.

"So, how do you know it's him?"

"Because he's confronted me in person as well. He's threatened me many times, and the words and phrases used in these texts—exactly the same. And Libby, I don't have any other enemies. I'm a well-respected professional in the community. But this guy—he's unhinged."

"Isn't that enough for the police?"

"You'd think … but they haven't caught him red-handed. Basically, he has to harm me before anything will be done."

"And he nearly did."

"Exactly."

"So, you were kicking Russ out?" I pull out the eviction notice, holding it up to read.

He hung his head. "I had to. The guy is a train wreck."

I wait, my eyes egging him on to tell me the entire story.

"First, he didn't show up with his wife like he said when I'd agreed to take them in."

"He didn't?" I decide not to let on that I know his wife.

"When he called asking me for help, I was hesitant. The guy is trouble. When he mentioned he was married, then I thought he'd changed things around and it might be okay to lend him a hand."

Martin offers me a drink, and I opt for a bottle of water.

"He showed up without the wife, and I was initially convinced she would join him within days. Well, a month went by … then two … and his excuses became more and more unbelievable. Honestly, Libby, I got to where I questioned whether she even existed, or perhaps something had happened to her."

"Oh, wow." I couldn't help wondering what Joanne's role was in this charade. After all, I'd seen them together on the video surveillance, yet her story to Willow and me had been that Russ left her long before she arrived in Arizona.

"Anyway, I only meant my offer for housing assistance to be short term all along, so I asked him how the house hunting was coming along. Of course, there was always the promise of moving out 'next week' followed by many excuses when it never happened."

He drinks from his coffee mug, staring into it before continuing.

"Then he started drinking. And I suspected some harder drugs as well based on his erratic behavior. That was always his thing, you know, and that's also when I knew I had to draw the line."

"How did he take that?"

"Well, I had to get an eviction notice, didn't I?"

"Any idea how the murder victim ended up with Russ' wallet in his pocket?"

"No idea. But clearly, they must have known each other."

I suggest we go to the police station with all the evidence and, between the two of us, we demand some answers as to why they're not pursuing Paul Sanchez, after these repeated threats.

CHAPTER THIRTY

Greg answers my call and agrees to pick up the twins from the community center once I convince him I am perfectly safe. I may or may not have led him to believe I was still at the hospital. In our time together, I've learned that he worries—so why worry him by telling the *whole* story?

I pull up behind Martin's GMC Denali at the police station and take a deep breath as I shut off the engine. This isn't my favorite place. To date, it's been difficult to get information, and I always seem to leave frustrated. Hopefully, this time will be different, I tell myself as I get out of my vehicle.

We walk inside and into the familiar cacophony. The few seats in the lobby hold an eclectic group of individuals who all looked *thrilled* to be there. The constant background of police radios squelching, and officers scattering about, makes me regret we ever walked through the doors.

"They don't have time for us," I mutter to Martin.

Whether he heard me, he steps forward to the desk asking to see Detective Rabideau. As soon as I hear the name, I picture the cold, but methodical woman who took my statement on the day of the murder. We strike out; it's her day off, but Detective Torres will be with us shortly.

"You haven't spoken with Officer Chesky?" I ask Marty.

"No, Rabideau and Torres handled my stalking case."

I am just about to suggest we ask for Chesky when the clean-cut, average-height, and muscular Torres takes us into one of the classic sterile rooms and asks us to take our seats.

"Good to see you again, Mr. Spiegel, Ms. Madsen. I'm a little surprised you're here together, but what brings you in today?"

I am surprised he remembered me by name.

"We'd like an update on the case, and we think we have more to share," I promptly offer.

"Oh, really? Come to confess?" The smug look on Torres' face was intentional.

Both Martin and I turn toward each other, horrified by the remark.

"We have nothing to confess, as you know." Martin clears his throat and calmly laces his fingers together, placing them in full view on the metal table. "I have credible evidence of who I suspect committed murder in my home. To date, I'm not being taken seriously."

I can't hold back. "Also, this whole situation could relate to another investigation currently happening in Heber."

Martin turns his head in my direction, his eyebrows lift and his eyes pointedly question mine.

Officer Torres jotted 'Heber' on his notepad. "Go on, Mr. Spiegel."

Martin starts a long story about how the justice system wronged him. I sit back diligently, but feel it's not the right approach. Always praise law enforcement if you want cooperation, I've learned. Still, I sit quietly and watch for clues about how I'll approach Torres.

When Martin takes a breather, I try sneaking in with further points. Torres silences me.

"I think both of you should know that we have used the information you've brought to us. Keep this in mind— it *is* an ongoing investigation; therefore, we're not at liberty to share information with you each and every time you call or show up at our doorstep."

Both of us start with, "But…"

Torres holds a hand up. "Please." He picks up his phone, types in something quickly, and then places it deliberately back onto the metal table. "We *do* have some information to share with you today."

All eyes look up when the door opens and in walk two other detectives: Munson and Sanders. They take up positions, standing along the wall opposite us and behind Torres.

"I'm sure you remember our detectives on this case. Both of you have had the pleasure of giving your statements to them. And yes, we've shared your *evidence*, Mr. Spiegel. Munson, Sanders, care to update our visitors with the latest?"

Detective Munson pushes his thick black-rimmed glasses up on his nose. "At approximately 0300 this morning, we served a search warrant and detained Paul Sanchez at his current residence in Montana." He gives Torres a signal, and the TV beside them on the wall lights up.

They play body-camera footage showing a no-knock entry into a residence. The SWAT team quickly moves through the darkness, then we see lights turn on, a barely awake and confused woman screaming, '*What's going on*?' She's taken aside, and then we witness two different men being handcuffed and hauled outside. The footage stops.

"That's definitely him," Martin mutters next to me. "Who are the others?"

"The residence belongs to Paul Sanchez's sister. The other man is her husband. Both of them are now detained for harboring a fugitive, but we expect the homeowners had no part in the murder of John Doe."

Confused, I stop him. "John Doe? You still don't know who Sanchez killed?"

Detective Sanders steps forward. "We've since learned that the DNA from John Doe wasn't a match with Russ Blankenship. Also, we did not find Spiegel's DNA on our John Doe. But Paul Sanchez was a direct match for evidence found at the scene, including DNA on the victim's body. We're sure we've detained the right guy. We're still seeking answers about the identity of John Doe."

"So, you've spoken to Russ then? He's alive?" This would be great news to share with Willow; I only pray she hasn't shared my incorrect presumptions from yesterday.

"We have not found him yet. But we're looking for him. We'd like to return his wallet."

Then I remember the storage unit theft. "Officer Chesky may have knowledge of his whereabouts from about a week ago—they have surveillance video."

"Thank you, Ms. Madsen. We'll reach out."

Another picture pops up on the screen. It was of the deceased. I gasp and quickly twist my body to face away. Detective Munson asks each of us if we can identify John Doe. With a quick glance, I say no. Marty tells them again he has never seen the man before. Soon after, we walk out of the station.

As we walk through the parking lot, I mention, "You must be relieved that they caught your stalker."

"Definitely." He lets out a sigh, then adds, "I sure hope you find the culprit who stole from the community center. If Russ was involved, I hope there's accountability for his actions, once and for all. For now, I'm happy he's out of my home."

"And I meant to tell you—his wife made it out West. She's the one I was visiting in the hospital. I've made friends with her and her sister. It appears she and Russ are in on that theft. It'll be interesting how that wraps up. Anyway, let me know if he shows up back on your doorstep."

Martin slows as he approaches his GMC. "Well, at least now I can get back to working without looking over my shoulder every two seconds for Paul Sanchez."

"You take care, Martin."

"Yep, you got it. Thanks, Libby."

We both get in our vehicles and wave to each other as we pull away from the police station in opposite directions. Seconds later, my phone rings. It's Willow.

"Libby, where are you? Joanne is awake, and you need to hear this."

CHAPTER THIRTY-ONE

Joanne and Willow are talking as I enter the room. The tension between them crackles like electricity. I break through it with a smile and a hello. Willow pulls over a chair so I can sit next to her.

"I guess Russ has been in the area this whole time," Willow informs me. "Joanne says she was a passenger in *his* truck when the accident happened."

I look directly at Joanne, who seems to cower into her covers. "I thought he was missing."

Willow curtly cuts in before Joanne can say anything. "Apparently, that was all a bunch of BS."

"Uh, I don't understand," I say, wanting to hear the story from Joanne even though I'm the only one in the room who has seen the surveillance video.

Willow doesn't give Joanne an opportunity to speak. "I'm still trying to understand this myself, trust me. But apparently, she and her husband have been thieving their way across the United States. When she called me, weeks back, I guess I ended up inviting their crimes right into our backyards."

"Joanne?" I look innocently for her explanation. "Is this true?"

She smooths her covers out with her hands. "I swear, Willow, I was *trying* to leave him. You don't know what he's like. I figured if I could get as far as Arizona, I'd be closer to you and I could ditch him and start a new life."

Before Willow launched in again, I held up my hand. "Wait, so you left Russ with his buddy Martin and called Willow for a place to stay? Why lie about Russ going missing?"

Both of them look at me, shell-shocked.

"How long have you known?" Willow asks me.

"I've pieced enough of it together, yes."

The patient hems and haws before hanging her head in shame. "Here's how it all went…" She reaches over for the cup on the nearby tray and takes a sip. "Remember, Libby, how I told you about the place he kept me in for years?"

Willow glances at me dumbfounded, and I nod hoping to keep Joanne talking. "Yes, I remember—and I thought you'd escaped from there and ended up here in Arizona."

Joanne gives a wistful look. "Yeah. Well, I might have insinuated that, but I only told you stories of the past and not about our life in recent years. Back then, I thought we were truly in love. For many months—I was, anyway. He went to work, and I kept up with the tiny home we'd made for ourselves out in the woods. Of course, I was trying to get pregnant, but never did. I'm thankful for that now, but at the time, it was devastating I couldn't give him the one thing he wanted."

"What type of work did Russ do?" I asked.

"Uh, he did a lot of stuff. Mechanics, and uh…"

"Stealing stuff," Willow adds with disdain. "He's a no-good, thieving slimebag!"

"Yeah, he sold stuff off when things were tight. I didn't ask a whole lot of questions. But it was always at the back of my mind. You know, from when I'd witnessed how he stole small stuff from the convenience stores before we settled down in the woods."

Cutting to the chase, I need to know. "Joanne, was Russ abusive?"

She hangs her head again. "He never hit me if that's what you're asking."

"Were you afraid of him?" I clarify.

"Very much so."

Willow scoffs. "Why didn't you leave then?"

I touch my friend's arm. "I'm sure it wasn't that easy. Is that right, Joanne?"

She nods. "I only wanted to make him happy. I swear I didn't know how scary he was until much more recently when…" She shivers and pulls her covers up over her arms.

"What happened, Joanne?"

"He gets this vacant look in his eyes—a darkness that is evil. I learned never to cross him. That's all."

Willow shifts in her seat impatiently. "So, what was the plan? You left the small home in the woods in Mississippi. For what? Why?"

Joanne shifts in the bed. "He came home one day all in a fury and said we had to leave. Rushing all around the house, he started throwing things into bags and shoved them into a new car he'd brought home. Said we needed to hurry, so I didn't question him and just did what he asked. Within the hour, we left our home and set out on the highway. At first, it was like an adventure. At least that's what I convinced myself of … you know, that it could be a good restart for us."

Joanne sniffles, grabs a tissue from the tray next to her and blows her nose. "But it all got so much worse." I watch as tears stream down her face.

I reach over and put a hand on hers. "How so?"

"I made the mistake of asking where he got the car and where we were going. He went ballistic. We argued for a while and, for whatever reason, I kept asking questions. Too many, I suppose."

We reach over to distract and stop her when she bangs her palm into her forehead, saying repeatedly, "Stupid, stupid, stupid!"

After another sip of water, she calms down again. "The next thing I knew, he pulled over and tossed me out of the car. I grabbed the bag I'd had at my feet, but that's all I had with me. I didn't see him again until about a week ago."

So many questions, and Willow and I compete in asking them.

"Where were you when he kicked you out?" I asked.

She explained that at the time she had no idea, but learned while hitchhiking that she was in West Texas.

"You hitchhiked all the way to Arizona?" Willow asks.

She nods. "No choice."

"Why didn't you call me then?"

Joanne gives Willow a skeptical look. "And say what? I felt horribly embarrassed about how my life had ended up.

It's still hard to admit all this and, besides, look how you're reacting now."

I step in. "Okay, so you wind up in Arizona. How did you know Willow was in Heber?"

Willow answers, "She called me when she made it to Phoenix. Only I believed she was still somewhere down south. She didn't say, and I didn't ask—I only assumed that."

Joanne nods in agreement. "I'm sorry. By this time, I was sure Russ had left me forever. I was still processing everything, and by the time I called you, I really only wanted to get back on my feet. No handouts, but I'd finally admitted to myself after sleeping, terrified, under too many bridges, that I needed a little help. That's when I called to see if I could come visit."

Willow interjects, "All this is great background, but Libby, this isn't the worst of it. Joanne stole the sculpture!"

Joanne protests.

"You did!" Willow shouts. "You said so yourself. So, just stop it!"

I remember watching the video surveillance and seeing Joanne and a tall man. Watching her now, I knew there was more to the story.

"Joanne, what happened? Why would you steal from the community center?"

"Libby, please believe me—it was *not* my idea, but I could not stop him."

"Stop who?"

"Russ."

"How did he find you?"

"I don't know." Huge crocodile tears stream down her face, and I hand her another tissue. "But I was feeling so lonely, so when we bumped into each other in town, I caved. I really believed he came looking for me because he loved me."

"And that's not the reason?"

She shakes her head and blows her nose again. "No. Somehow, he learned I was staying with Willow and volunteering at the community center. There was something he mentioned—I can't remember exactly what right now—that sent chills up my spine. He had been stalking me for days before we actually ran into each other."

"What did he want?"

Joanne looks at me confused.

"You said you figured out he wasn't here because he loved you—so, why was he here?"

"Oh! He'd made some friends in Show Low. Apparently, one of them knew of a well-known artist who donated a really expensive sculpture to the community center for the silent auction. He came over to Heber with that person under the pretense that he was interested in the art." She scoffs, shaking her head. "He doesn't know the first thing about art!"

"But I guess he saw me volunteering at the community center when he arrived. I never saw him, but anyway, someone there told him that the sculpture was being stored offsite. I learned later that he'd followed you and Willow to the storage unit that day." She stops and I see her look of contemplation.

"What is it, Joanne? Did you just remember something else?"

She nods. "That *was* the day I ran into him! Because that night, he took me to the storage unit. He told me it was his friend's unit, and he was picking something up for him. He had the keys—I helped him load and then he dropped me off outside Willow's home and said he had to get the delivery finished but he'd call me in the morning."

"You honestly didn't know this was the stolen sculpture we'd all been talking about?" Willow stands, pacing the floor, on the other side of the hospital bed. "C'mon, Joanne!"

She shakes her head adamantly. "No! And it's not like you told me anything about what was going on. How would I know?"

I try to remember if I'd shared anything with Joanne about the theft, but can't remember exactly. I agreed with Willow though; I thought everyone associated with the community center knew it was missing this whole time. *Why wouldn't Joanne speak up and say something?*

I check my watch, anxious, knowing I am missing spending the whole day with my family back in Heber.

"One more question—where were you and Russ going when this accident occurred?"

Sighing, she answers in a soft voice. "I thought he was taking me home to our cozy home in the woods. Back to Mississippi. I thought we were going to start over and he'd changed things around. He told me he'd been working as a mechanic in Show Low for months and had saved a bunch of money. I believed he wanted me back, and we were finally going home."

"But something happened, didn't it?"

The hollow look behind her eyes tells me all I needed to know. "He wanted to silence me."

Willow and I quiver as she explains how the darkness enveloped him again when she started asking him questions. She asked where he got the nice new black truck with all the bells and whistles, and admitted she knew every word that came from his mouth was a lie. She couldn't help herself, so she called him out on his lies, and they started arguing. At some point in the argument, she grabbed the wheel with all the force she could muster, and they went sailing. After that, everything went dark.

CHAPTER THIRTY-TWO

I can't get Joanne's words out of my head for the entire drive home. *He tried to silence me.* Even though Willow is still skeptical of Joanne's story, I believe her. I think she got caught up under his spell. I pictured the meek woman trying to stand up against someone his size. She risked her own life in a horrific accident just to get away from him, which was a chilling fact.

Ruminating on the day's revelations, I now know the police arrested Paul Sanchez, the coin donor and suspected murderer. Martin Spiegel was safe and sound, but luckily, he hadn't been home or he would have been the victim. But who was John Doe? And where was Russ Blankenship now?

Hadn't I heard about someone from the car accident

being airlifted to Phoenix? I ask Siri to call my buddy Officer Chesky. Maybe he'd have some answers?

When it goes to voicemail, I leave a message asking about the accident and whether they know the identity of the driver. I share how I believe it was Russ Blankenship, and they really need to talk to his wife, Joanne, who is still in the hospital. Hanging up, I feel good about doing my part to help.

Greg, Shadow, and the girls are out in the yard when I pull up.

"Aunt Libby!" Annie calls out. "You have to see this!"

I leave my stuff in the car and run off with Annie.

"See what Uncle Greg did?" She points upward, and I see many strings of fairy lights strung along from the back patio all the way over to the guest house.

Greg blushes and gives me a welcome hug. "I love that she's already calling me Uncle Greg," he whispers in my ear while kissing it. Pulling away, he looks at the lights. "Did I get it right? Do they look similar to how you wanted them?"

"Perfect!" I stand tall on my toes and plant another kiss on his cheek.

Apple shows me how she helped by handing Uncle Greg the strings of lights up on the ladder. "Wait until nighttime. These are going to be so pretty!"

That evening, we sit out on the patio, grill burgers and enjoy the mild last days of summer weather. As soon as it gets dark, Annie flips the switch for the lights, and it is magical.

"Can you picture it now? All the chairs set up on the grass over there under the lights. And soon we'll get the arch up; that's where you and I will take our vows."

"I can't wait, Mr. Lawson."

"Ugh, you two…" Apple grimaces.

Shadow licks Apple's hand when she isn't watching. "Oh gross!" She stomps off into the house to clean up, and Shadow hoovers up all the crumbs she's dropped.

Greg leans over. "So, all that business in Show Low is taken care of then?"

I had filled him in on some details earlier, but had tried to keep everything from the girls' ears. Annie's head perks up from her plate at Greg's question now, so I keep my answer simple. "Yes. Joanne is going to be okay. I think Willow said she'll be released in another day or two."

"Will we get to see Willow before we leave tomorrow?" Annie asks me.

"I hope so. But I'm not sure yet."

"We had so much fun with her. Can we come here again next summer?"

Greg and I both answer. "I sure hope so!"

"I'm not sure what our plans will be, but if we're here, then you girls are certainly welcome."

"The boys too," Greg adds.

I give Greg the 'careful what you wish for' look at the same time Annie groans.

Apple's voice startles me from behind. "Hey Aunt Libby, after we make our s'mores and then help you clean up, can Annie and I stay in the guest house tonight?"

I hadn't considered that. "What do you think, Greg?"

"I don't see why not."

"Yay!!" the twins shout in unison.

By the time we get the girls all set up in the guest house, I am beat and ready to sit with my feet up and enjoy a show on TV with my fiancé. Greg starts the gas fireplace, and I pop some popcorn in the microwave. Shadow follows my every move, hoping I'll drop some pieces for her.

We are thirty minutes into our movie when I notice a truck pull up.

"Are you expecting someone?" I ask Greg.

"Nope." He walks to the window and peers out. "It looks like it's Ted."

My spirits sink as I really want quiet time this evening. Greg steps outside onto the front porch, and I vaguely hear portions of their conversation. The door opens, Greg's head pops in and he says he's going to help Ted and should be back within an hour.

"Okay. I'll probably just read then—in bed."

"Sorry. But it shouldn't take long."

Shadow and I walk out back, and I use my keys to let myself into the guest house. The girls are sitting on their sleeping bags in the middle of the floor telling ghost stories.

"Just wanted to say goodnight. Need anything before I head to bed?"

Both of them shake their heads, and I turn to leave.

"Wait, Aunt Libby, could Shadow stay with us tonight?" Apple asks.

Annie tilts her head. "It might be these ghost stories, but now we keep hearing bumps in the night. Shadow will protect us from the ghosts."

I chuckle at the precocious teens. "Okay. I think Shadow would love that." Her tail whips around. Whether she actually knew she was being left with them was unclear. "Her water bowl is in my therapy room. Make sure it's still full, please. Also, I'll leave her leash right here in case she needs to go out for potty later." I set it on the accent table just inside the door.

The girls stare at me, taking in my instructions, and probably don't realize there is more to caring for a dog than just having one in the room for comfort.

"Good night," I say to all the girls as I close the door behind me.

A brisk wind blew, giving a distinct fall-like feel to the air and sending a chill through me. I hurry across the yard and back inside the house, shutting off the lights and seeking peaceful refuge in my bed with a good mystery in hand. After the third time I dropped the book onto my chest, I surrendered, turning off the bedside lamp, and falling fast asleep.

A thunderous crash jolts me out of bed. I reach for a bat that I routinely keep next to the bed. My head whips from right to left, only it was too dark to see well. I notice on the clock, it is 11:42. Greg is not in bed. I creep down the hallway, expecting to find that he's knocked something over, trying to walk through the house in the dark.

I call out, "Greg?"

Silence.

I stand with my back against the hallway wall and listen carefully. *What woke me up?*

Silence.

Where is Greg?

I slip through the living room, my eyes adjusting to the darkness. Everything is in place, exactly as I'd left it a couple of hours before. I turn the corner into the kitchen and flip on the light, blinding myself.

Blinking away the sharp contrast from darkness, I look around the room, only to find everything undisturbed. I step to the back door and check the locks before breathing a sigh of relief—must have been a bad dream. After a second or two, I turn on the hallway light, turn off the kitchen lighting, and make my way back to the bedroom.

I check my phone for a message from Greg, but there isn't one. Tiredness takes over again, and I turn out the light in an attempt to sleep. *What's taking Greg so long?* I worry for a moment, but quickly drift back into dream mode.

Then I hear another loud noise. This time there is no mistaking—it was a girl's scream.

CHAPTER THIRTY-THREE

I bolt out of my bed, grabbing the bat and my phone as I sprint down the hallway, turning on lights along the way. I push a chair out of my way, running through the dining area and kitchen. Fumbling with the lock, I throw the door open and charge through the backyard. No lights are on in the guest house, but I hear barking and I hear crying.

I forgot the keys!

Banging on the door, I scream, "Apple! Annie! Open up!"

The sounds inside cease. I listen for a second. "What's going on girls? Open up!"

The door slowly creaks open, but all I see is darkness inside. I reach out to open the door wider but something's blocking it.

"What's happening, Apple? Annie?"

"Don't come in, Aunt Li...." One of them screams at the exact moment I feel enormous pressure on my arm and I'm flung into the living area.

"Nice of you to join us, Aunt Libby," a male voice hisses.

Every fiber of my being is alert; a piercing pain shoots through my hip. I quickly use my hands and feet to crawl backwards toward the sofa. Darkness envelopes the room, making it difficult to see where anyone is, except I hear the two girls whimpering nearby and there is a bulky presence hovering over me.

"Joanne said this was a nice place. I thought I'd come check it out for myself." The gravelly voice was one I didn't recognize. "I mean, I should come meet the woman who had her hands all over my wife, right?"

"It wasn't like that... I'm a..." I squeak out.

His thunderous laugh startles me; I flinch. "I know what you are!"

"Okay, okay." I try to use a calm voice. "Who are you?"

"I think you know already."

"Whatever you want with me, please let my nieces go. They have nothing to do with this."

"Ah, but they do. They're leverage—and quite good ones at that."

"Russ, I'm sure we can talk this through."

"Ah, ha! You know exactly who I am. Well, then, you're right; let's get down to business."

He grabs my hair and pulls me across the room, heading down the short hallway toward my therapy room. "Girls, RUN!"

I can't see them, or know whether it's even possible for

them to get out. Pain pierces my skull when he slugs me and tosses me into the room. My body slumps like a rag doll.

"You think you can poison my woman's mind and get away with it?"

His words muffle together. My brain feels almost underwater, with an intense pounding in my ears.

"I don't…" my throat closes up when I feel a boot on my backside.

The throaty voice was now right on top of my ear. "You and that sister of hers!"

"What?" I mutter. "I really don't know…"

"Stop it! Stop your lying. I know you have been poking your nose around in our business. I saw you slinking around Show Low. And I watched her come here to your place several times. *You* are the reason she got it in her head to leave me!"

He gives another kick.

"Owww!" I scream.

I feel him pacing the room, but I only see his shadow from a sliver of moonlight shining through the window. The tension exudes from his body, and I curl tighter into the fetal position protecting myself from the next blow.

Instead, he continues pacing. Cursing wildly and telling his own tales.

"Yeah, I saw you all right. And it would have worked perfectly if you'd minded your own business and stopped involving the police. I should have run you over the first time I saw you out jogging with your annoying dog."

"I don't understand." *And where's Shadow now? Why wasn't she here biting this ogre?*

"I was supposed to be dead! Then no one would be

looking for me now."

"Oh. In Mr. Spiegel's home?"

His evil laugh makes me pull my knees in tighter. "*Mr. Spiegel* . . . listen to you. Yeah, I saw you palling around with my friend, too."

"Your friend said Joanne was never with you when you arrived at his house. Why was that?"

"I ask the questions around here!" he bellowed.

Being bolder, I add, "Ohhh! *You* left your wallet in the dead guy's pocket? *You* wanted them to think it was you."

He hisses, "Of course I did. I didn't want to be linked to that schmuck. What an idiot he was! Thought he was all tough when I carjacked him for his sweet ride. Well, he ain't so tough now, is he?"

A noise outside catches both of our attention. He leaves the room, and I try my hardest to move, but can't get anything to work.

"Ah shit, the girls got themselves untied!" I hear from the other room.

He comes back in, runs right up to me and kicks me again, this time in my shin.

Crying, I shout, "Stop it! What do you want?"

"I want my wife back!"

"I don't have her—why are you doing this to *me?*"

This time I hear the distinct sound of a car door slamming. Both optimism and dread fill my brain. *Greg is home. Distract this thug.*

"How do you know Joanne lived through that awful accident?"

"Because I saw her sitting up and talking in her hospital bed." His voice drips with disdain.

My heart pounds, realizing he got that close to her again.

"How did *you* make it unscathed in the accident?"

"Well, that's the million-dollar question, isn't it?" he says mockingly.

"I thought they airlifted you to a hospital in Phoenix."

"That was the other driver—poor guy."

I recoil at his merciless demeanor. *Where is Greg? Where are the girls?*

"So, what's your plan, Russ? How am I supposed to help you get Joanne back?"

His attention went to the front of the guesthouse again.

I raise my voice. "What is it I'm supposed to help you with? You think killing me or my family will make Joanne feel differently about you?"

Russ' shadow moves so quickly, I can't react. He grips my arm forcefully, and I'm sure he'll break it. With remarkable ease, he drags me out of the room, stands me up, holding me tight against him.

The guesthouse windows fill with red and blue strobes. That's when I clearly see his gun for the first time. The terror rises into my throat as I realize I'm a hostage smack in the middle of so much weaponry.

CHAPTER THIRTY-FOUR

Come out with your hands up!" a cop shouts with a bullhorn.

Russ promptly kicks the front door closed, hustles us backwards, never releasing his death grip around my body. A flurry of activity begins outside. I hear officers mounting the steps to the front patio, and I presume they've surrounded the entire place.

His hoarse voice hisses, "Those damn kids! I should have killed them immediately."

"Russ, none of this ends well for you."

"Wrong!" he grunts. "This doesn't end well for *you*."

"What if we ask the police to bring Joanne to you?"

His tight grip softens briefly.

"Seriously. If that's what you want, I'll explain everything was a misunderstanding tonight and you only want to see your wife."

His excruciatingly powerful arms quickly obliterate my moment of optimism. I can't breathe.

"Do you think I'm an idiot?"

I try shaking my head. "Of course not," I choke out. "But I can't breathe here."

He drags me to the sofa and drops me heavily, face first. Pulling zip ties from his back pocket, he tightens them around my wrists and ankles, leaving me face down on the couch. Praying the cops don't pound the door down, shooting, as I'm merely feet inside the door, I try pleading with Russ again.

"Listen. Can we at least attempt to negotiate with the cops? I think if I can talk to them, I can make them understand."

His cell phone rings in his pocket. I watch as he pulls it out and stares with confusion.

"It's them, isn't it?" I prod. "See, they're willing to negotiate. That's how it works. Answer it."

He pushes the button. "What."

This guy sure needs some lessons in pleasantries, I think to myself.

Staying still, listening to see if I can catch what the other person is saying, I hear my name. Then, I think I overhear the word 'demands', but otherwise, everything jumbles and Russ doesn't make it any easier for me as he paces around.

I stretch my neck, looking at each window, and notice all the blinds are down so no one can see inside. Twisting, and trying not to groan outwardly when the ties cut into my skin, I catch a glance of the window nearest my feet. The blinds don't reach the windowsill, and even though my eyes had adjusted to the dark, I find it difficult to see out. I blink several times, concentrating really hard. *There is someone looking in!*

"No way! This is all a trick—you're going to shoot me the second I open the door."

I blink at the eyes staring at me. *Can they see me?* I move my head trying to point toward the back rooms—there is a door back there, but how do I communicate that with only my eyes?

"If you guys don't leave now, I'm going to kill her and then I'll start shooting all of you!" His irritation progressively grows, and I want to cry.

When I look back at the window, the person is gone. *My only lifeline to the outside — and they left!* Now, tears stream down both cheeks, pooling on the sofa fabric beneath me.

He throws his phone, and it smashes into the kitchenette, causing me to jump. All at once, everything seems to escalate. He picks up items within his reach and throws them against the wall. I do my best to pull a pillow over my head as the shrapnel from various objects falls all around me—glass, plastic, books.

During his tirade, I'm sure I hear a noise at the rear of the building. I close my eyes, bracing myself and expecting live fire, but then hear crazy screams, thuds, and more items crashing. I find myself humming to drown it all out; rocking back and forth to soothe my nerves. *How long will this terror go on?* The thrumming in my ears sounds oddly like growls and snarls, but I don't dare open my eyes.

Continuing to rock back and forth, I feel something at the elbow—warm and wet. I hum louder. A firm hand grabs my shoulder, and I howl.

"Libby…" a gentle voice says.

I kick out with my bound-up legs, then try to karate-chop my bound arms toward my assailant.

"Libby! It's okay. It's Ted. We got him. Hey, it's okay." He scoops me up in his strong arms and I hear Shadow's bark. I open my eyes and see the gentle giant when I look up. I twist my head around and see Shadow following. *Such a good girl.*

Ted carries me outside. The bright lights all around are too much, but then I see Greg running toward us.

"Someone, bring a knife! Scissors! Something!" Greg yells.

Ted carries me over to the back patio of the main house, telling us both how Shadow got to the bad guy right before he did. "She lit right into him—his legs are good and tore up!"

Greg cuts off the ties, pulling me close to him. "Oh, honey, I'm so sorry."

We hold onto each other, and I sob with relief. Police are everywhere, yet I can't let go of Greg. I've never been so happy to see him. Then, Shadow pounces on us and licks away my tears. The cops bring the twins over to us, and we all go inside the house where we give our statements.

CHAPTER THIRTY-FIVE

Pancakes were exactly what the doctor ordered when I woke up all bruised and stiff. Greg got up early with the twins, and they had a full brunch on display when I hobbled into the kitchen.

Again, I pull the girls into my arms and, although it hurts, I squeeze them so hard. "I love you two, and I'm so grateful you didn't get injured."

"We're fine, Aunt Libby. But, you … well, you look awful!" Annie says, squinching up her face.

"Gee, thanks!" I chuckle as I take a seat at the breakfast bar and accept the vanilla latte from Greg. The girls sit on either side of me. "What's all this?" My eyes take in the enormous pile of pancakes, which Greg was still adding to, hot off the griddle. Then, there were bowls of fresh berries, a plate of crispy bacon, and warm syrup.

"We made your favorites!" Apple exclaims.

My heart swells. "I sure wish you two could stay longer.

I feel bad I kept getting pulled away. And of course, I feel horrible about the disturbed man last night."

"That's not your fault. And we want to stay, too. But I have camp to get to, and Annie starts band practice next week."

"Where did the summer go?"

Everyone shrugs while watching Greg toss more cakes on the pile.

"Listen, girls, we need to give your mom a *gentle* explanation of what happened last night. Should we discuss what that might sound like?"

Both of them vehemently shake their heads. "Don't tell Mom *anything*! She'll never let us come here again!" they say in unison.

I catch Greg staring at me, just waiting for my reaction.

"Um, I'm not sure…" I say, when the doorbell rings and we all know it's Jordan.

Annie runs for the door, and I hear her ushering her mother inside. "Mom, we had soooo much fun," she exaggerates and eyes each one of us dramatically as they walk into the kitchen. "Didn't we, Apple?"

Her sister raves over all the fun stuff they did, but both girls mostly play up the volunteer work at the community center and all the people they met as being their favorite parts. "We want to do it again sometime!"

Greg and I invite Jordan to have a seat, and we all enjoy breakfast while the girls talk nonstop about how great Heber is. By the time they finish breakfast, the girls pull my sister off to their room to gather their belongings. Before we know it, we find ourselves saying goodbye from the windows of their Subaru.

I figured it out, standing there waving as they drove away. Those girls had played us. They simply never gave us a second alone, or a chance to get a word in edge-wise, to have an adult conversation with their mother. I stood there shaking my head in disbelief—very clever teenagers.

CHAPTER THIRTY-SIX

Willow made it home several days later. Heartbroken that her sister was in custody, but eager to get back to her own life, she came to me for a massage. During her tabletop confession, she gives me the lowdown on everything Joanne had confessed since the last time I saw them.

Since learning of Russ' arrest, Joanne cooperated fully with law enforcement. Willow still hopes she'll be able to plea for lesser charges, but regardless, Joanne was an accomplice and she is in a lot of trouble.

I have conflicted feelings about Willow's sister, but one thing is for sure: they put my family in harm's way, so I'll never get over that.

"I understand Russ is a lifelong criminal and we may never know the *why* behind everything, but I'll never quite understand why he involved my family in all this."

"I think only because you'd gotten close to Joanne,"

Willow guesses.

"So, if I understand you correctly, Russ stole some guy's truck. A skirmish must have happened, and he ends up killing the guy. Why leave him at Marty's home?"

"Oh, I think I know. Apparently, after stealing the truck, Russ drove back to Marty's, packing up his belongings, and planning to hit the road again. A neighbor mentioned someone in a blue Subaru in the area, and that person linked back to the stolen truck. Anyway, I guess things escalated, Russ stabbed the guy and left him for dead, also, leaving his wallet to make the police believe he was the one who died."

"That's sickening," I groan, remembering how terrifying Russ was and how close he came to seriously harming me.

"No kidding. So glad Joanne got away from him."

"It sounded like she wanted to go with him, though."

"Well, until she remembered and saw his dark side again. Like she told us, she knew she had to do something drastic to get away from him. That nearly cost her life."

"Too bad it hadn't cost him his." I still shudder to think what could have happened that night at our home. The twins! "Hey, did Joanne ever say anything about Kevin—that high school football player? Was he involved in helping steal the sculpture?"

"No. Not at all. She laughed, though, at your suspicions there may have been something untoward."

"You should have seen the looks exchanged between them!"

"I think she gave him cigarettes on the sly."

"Ohhh," I chuckled, seeing how that made more sense. "Guess she and Ted aren't going any further with that flirtation either."

"Nope. I saw him at The Mill last night. Poor guy, he needs to catch a break."

"Yeah. What is his deal?"

"Oh, he has a hard time keeping women around. And it's a shame because he's such a friendly fellow. I think he's just a little set in his ways."

"And maybe a little scary sometimes?"

"No! He's a giant teddy bear. Maybe a little misunderstood sometimes, though."

"Well, what about the guy he beat up at The Mill?"

"Yeah, I don't know what got into him that night."

"I know. It felt like it came out of nowhere."

"Well, one thing I know about Ted is that he's very protective."

That reminded me of how he had saved my life. He said Shadow did, but I was sure it was both of them.

Later that evening, Greg takes me out for a nice dinner at The Mill. As soon as we walk through the doors, we see Ted bellied up at the bar.

"Let's ask him to join us," I suggest to Greg.

"Good idea." He goes over to grab Ted, while I get us on the list to be seated.

Once we're at our table, I thank Ted again for coming to our rescue. "You'll never know how much it means to me."

"To us." Greg tilts his beer bottle and clinks it with his friend's drink.

"Ah shucks, guys. I'd do anything for you."

We each order our meals, and then Ted says something that stuns both of us.

"You know, the guy at your place that night was the

same one who attacked one of our cocktail servers here. Shelby—right over there."

Greg set his beer down. "What? That guy you decked the last time we were here?"

"Yep, same one."

Goosebumps formed on my forearms thinking about it. *Had he been that close all along?* "You know, he was Joanne's husband?" I asked Ted.

"Yeah. Dodged a bullet there." He took a swig of his beer. "I don't understand why I'm always attracted to the wrong type—but I am."

We listened to Ted's tales from many years of dating and several engagements, too. By the end of the evening, I agreed with Willow's assessment. Ted Bolton was a charming gentleman. We'd have to help him out in screening his next love interest.

In the meantime, we had our own wedding to plan.

What's next for Libby and Shadow?
We may be hearing wedding bells … unless a new mystery gets in the way. Only time, and the imagination of award-winning author Jennifer J. Morgan, will tell!

Don't miss Book 12 in this "impressively original and deftly crafted"* series!
**Midwest Book Review*

* * *

Thank you for taking the time to read *Silent Shadows*. If you enjoyed it please tell your friends, and I would be so grateful if you would consider posting a review. Word of mouth is an author's best friend, and very much appreciated.
Thank you,
Jennifer Morgan

* * *

Acknowledgements

Thank you to everyone who keeps following Libby and her friends on their adventures. It's so much fun to write and I remain cheered on by all your words of encouragement. I'm blessed to have fans like you!

I'm also grateful to have family and friends who keep me motivated and pouring myself into these mysteries—I honestly couldn't imagine doing anything else. And, a super huge shout out to my beta readers: Gabi Hoffknecht, Susan Gross, Dawn Hasiotis, Isobel Tamney, Paula Webb, and Marcia Koopmann. You all have such thoughtful suggestions and each catch uniquely different mistakes. I truly appreciate your help.

Books in the Libby Madsen Cozy Mysteries series:

Shadows in the Forest
Spa Shadows
Shadowed Treasures
Shadow Retreats
Spooky Shadows
Shadow's Christmas Wish
Festive Shadows
Shadows in Alaska
Shadows Over Thanksgiving
Ghostly Amethyst Shadows
Silent Shadows
The Christmas Fairy – a holiday novella

Let's connect!

Website: jenniferjmorgan.com
Email: jennifer@jenniferjmorgan.com
Find me on Facebook, Twitter (X), BookBub, and Goodreads

Get a free book from Jennifer—scan the QR code to find out how!

www.ingramcontent.com/pod-product-compliance
Lightning Source LLC
Chambersburg PA
CBHW061602100726
47898CB00002B/493